Wynona and The Dragon

Wynona and The Dragon

James C Tillman

Published by
Big Yellow Dog LLC

Big Yellow Dog LLC
465 Linden St. Winnetka, Il 60093
Bigyellowdog@outlook.com

ISBN: 0986122610
ISBN 13: 9780986122613
Library of Congress Control Number: 2015902519
Big Yellow Dog LLC, Winnetka, IL

Dedication

To my true life partner Cheri. Without whom Wynona and the Dragon would never have seen the light of day. Your beautiful spirit has awakened my voice.

Acknowledgments

I wish to acknowledge Dr. Nathan Jacobs for the initial idea which inspired me to write Wynona and the Dragon.

I also wish to thank Donna Berg for her careful and excellent editing of this book.

Contents

1

Wynona

SKIPPING DOWN THE forest path, she gazed up at giant old-growth trees whose roots were locked in craggy, moss-covered rocks. Her raven hair bounced as she jumped from rock to rock while wishing that she was one of the many forest birds that hopped from branch to branch. She stopped to admire the sunlight filtering through the leaves as it fell on the forest floor and made a patchwork quilt of shade and light that moved rhythmically, as if conducted by the gentle breeze high up in the canopy. Peace filled her little heart, and the softness of the forest refreshed her young soul. Abruptly, a lovely flower on the path grabbed her attention, which then quickly shifted to a multicolored butterfly that lightly danced on the breeze above her head. She danced with it, running and jumping in perfect coordination while the butterfly delicately flitted and came to rest on the flower. The little girl carefully approached her new friend and studied its wise face. She felt like it was about to speak. Slowly, almost imperceptibly, the coolness of the forest altered; the forest was growing warmer. The little girl first noticed the change when a hot gust of wind whipped up behind her and sent the butterfly careening off the flower and into the distance. She stood there and watched it fade until it disappeared. Suddenly, a flash illuminated the forest, and she turned to see a brilliant light behind her. The air had also changed from the sweet aroma of growing things to the acrid smell of burning vegetation. Terror gripped her, and she ran, desperate to find safety from the approaching maelstrom. Her little legs flew down the path, but rocks and roots seemed to rise with malevolent intent to hinder her escape. The faster she ran, the more she was pitched down and scraped and bruised—only to rise again and again. Panic engulfed her as the fiery holocaust drew nearer. Once more, she tumbled face forward into the dirt as suffocating black smoke and hot embers surrounded her. She lifted her head and opened her eyes only to see the branches above bursting into mammoth fireballs and raining down upon her like Sodom and Gomorrah. She screamed and then...

Wynona bolted upright, gasping for air and slowly coming to awareness. She opened her tightly shut eyes and turned to look at the clock radio on her bed stand. The time was 6:45. She turned to the other side of the bed and saw an empty, head-sized impression on the pillow; the covers were turned back. She murmured an expletive and then looked back to the clock. A wave of realization came over her face, and she again let fly an expletive—this time louder and nastier. She jumped out of bed and ran to the bathroom.

Her eyes were slowly adjusting to the light when she caught her image in the mirror. She hated the first look at her reflection; it was always painful to see her hair pushed about her head like some small nocturnal creature had made its home there. Then there was her face—all blotched in the places she had slept on. But worse than her outward appearance was the fact that the first look at herself was somehow more frightful for its naked honesty. Here she stood in the glaring bathroom light—no painted-on smile and no well-honed look of indifference; all that would come after the first cup of coffee. This was the first naked view of her exposed soul. But what was most terrifying was what happened when the person in the mirror looked back. That person possessed a cold weariness that would have been expected from someone in a nursing home waiting to die.

She dreaded to see herself so unprotected every morning, and so she set about the business of putting on her public face.

Wynona was twenty-six years old, and when stretched to her full height, she barely hit five-foot-two. She was, as her father used to say, sweet and petite. However, that was something he said when she was seven; nothing about Wynona could now be considered sweet, except her outward appearance. She looked like the perfect embodiment of the girl next door. Old ladies regularly came up to pinch her rosy cheeks, and young men longed to gaze into her soft brown eyes. Her brown hair, once combed, flowed with a luster that invited fingertips. But therein lay the contradiction with Wynona. For all her outward appearance as a soft and gentle creature, she had a hardness to her that would not hesitate to emotionally disembowel anyone who dared to show her less than the level of respect she believed she was due. More than one young man who thought she was a tasty morsel had choked on her razor-sharp quills.

She glanced down and saw a blue toothbrush on the edge of the sink. Wynona's eyes flashed and her face contorted as she stared at it with a fierceness that came only to those whose anger is regularly employed. She pitched it in the toilet. All her next moves were well choreographed to make the exit from her apartment as quick as possible.

She was in the elevator and out the front door of her building within twenty minutes of waking up. She passed her doorman, whom she did not know, and caught a bus full of the same people she had shared the ride with for the past two years—whom she also did not know—past a city full of stores, lights, and residents that she didn't notice. Her attention was focused on her notebook computer, and it told her everything she needed to know about the world and her day's activities.

Wynona lived in a large city filled with what she considered small people, and she was determined to be the exception. Soon after graduation from college, she took a job at Smyth and Company, a marketing firm located in a tall glass skyscraper in the middle of the city. She had worked there for two years and in that brief time had managed to get herself promoted from junior account representative to associate account representative, a feat that normally took the especially ambitious employee five years to accomplish. Wynona always exceeded everyone's expectations except her own.

The bus ride was fourteen blocks and took exactly twenty minutes. During the short trip, Wynona was able to answer five e-mails, review two reports, and check her schedule. It was then that she realized that a sales meeting was called for 7:30 a.m., a full half hour before she was usually at her desk. A combination of frustration and anger overcame her as she snapped her laptop closed and threw it into her bag to prepare for the half-block sprint to her office building. It was exactly 7:45 when she rushed past the reception desk, where Mary, the receptionist, barely caught a glimpse of her and shouted, "They're in conference room A." When she reached her desk, Wynona shouldered her bag, grabbed her client notebook and purse, and flew down the hallway, all while conjuring some excuse that wouldn't be too lame to explain her tardiness.

The conference room was long and narrow with windows on both sides. One set of windows faced the hallway, while the other side looked out upon a spectacular view of the city from the sixty-fourth floor. In the center of the room was a one-piece mahogany table that was made especially for the room and was so large it had to be placed in the building while it was being constructed. Wynona had to walk the full length of the windows in sight of all in the conference room before she could enter—something she'd always referred to as "the walk of shame." She never failed to draw attention to a late coworker, and now that was exactly what she was experiencing. The irony of this was completely lost to her because humility was not an attribute that Wynona cultivated. As she approached the windows, all she could do was take a deep breath, look straight ahead, and walk with her most determined and forceful stride.

At the head of the table opposite the entrance door was Mr. Donald Smyth, CEO. He was a man in his midsixties with a receding hairline and advancing waistline. He had taken over the running of the company from his father ten years ago and since then had gone through one bypass and two marriages. The company was his life, and he made very sure that everyone who worked there knew that they were expected to have the same commitment to their work. That was why a fifteen-minute meeting infraction was not passed over any more than losing a $15 million account.

Wynona stepped into the conference room, quickly scanned for a vacant seat, and found, to her displeasure, the only seat left was next to Mr. Smyth. So she took another walk of shame all the way to the head of the table and as quickly as possible took the empty seat. Mr. Smyth was speaking and made no notice of her, for which she was immensely relieved. She opened up her client notebook and began to take notes.

"Glad you could join us, Ms. Swanson. I hope you didn't find the seven thirty start time too inconvenient." At this, Mr. Smyth removed his glasses and turned to Wynona with a stare that was meant to communicate contempt, but which more nearly approximated the look of someone who was trying to pass gas. That in itself would have caused Wynona to laugh if she had not been so full of self-condemnation.

"Sorry, sir. Please forgive my tardiness." Here she reached for the best excuse she could come up with under the circumstances. "My bus had a flat tire." Somewhere in the room there was a muffled laugh, and Wynona's eyes flashed with wounded pride while she looked to see who would dare doubt her fictitious excuse. As her eyes scanned the room, she realized it had come from Sean Pendleton, and her anger grew exponentially. Sean was a six-foot-two-inch, too-good-looking man in his early thirties with the body of an athlete and the mind and emotional intelligence of an adolescent. He too was an associate account representative, but it had taken him the usual five years to achieve this role—a fact that Wynona never ceased to enjoy reminding him of. He was also her "almost" boyfriend. Almost, because Wynona didn't attach herself to anyone or anything. She valued her independence more than life and was obsessed with controlling everyone and everything that composed her world. This meant that if anyone were to come into her world, they needed to obey her rules. That included Sean.

The meeting settled into a semblance of normalcy as Mr. Smyth droned on about the importance of closing sales. Wynona breathed a silent sigh and began to believe that her morning's missteps were now behind her. It was then that she heard the sound of faint but distinguishable music. Everyone in the room froze, for they knew what it was—the dreaded ringtone of an unsilenced cell phone, yet another unforgivable violation of meeting etiquette. To make matters worse, it wasn't even hip music. It was the theme song for the Wicked Witch of the West from the *Wizard of Oz*. Wynona let out a short gasp, and her mind raced to remember if she had turned off her ringer before the meeting, but then logic stepped in as she reasoned to herself that no one else would have that ringtone and no one else would be calling her before 8:00 a.m. but her own mother. Wynona lunged for her bag, dug through layers of stuff, and finally grabbed the phone with a grip that would have subdued a poisonous snake. She turned off the ringer, placed the phone next to her notebook, and attempted a thin smile.

"Do you have any more musical numbers for us, Ms. Swanson? Perhaps you would like to lead us all in a chorus of 'Ding Dong, the Witch Is Dead'?" And once again, Mr. Smyth gave her what he considered a withering look, but which only made him look exceedingly withered.

"No, sir" was all Wynona could mutter as she again buried her head in her notebook and again heard a slightly louder chuckle from Sean. Mercifully, there were no other major incidents during the meeting, unless she counted when her phone, which she had in her haste set to vibrate, went off. But she had whisked it into her lap before it was

too noticeable. When she looked down at it, the screen read Mom…
again!

The meeting came to its usual anticlimactic end, and the partici-
pants began filing out—after the grand exit of Mr. Smyth, of course.
Wynona wanted nothing more than to return to the safety of her
desk, gather herself, and lick her wounds. She made eye contact with
no one and feigned writing in her notebook till she was confident
she would have an unrestricted path to the door. She was just about
to escape from the room when Sean stepped into the doorway and
blocked her exodus. He apparently had been waiting just outside the
door for this opportunity to catch her in an uncharacteristically vulnerable state.

"Nice meeting, huh?" Wynona lifted her eyes to meet his with a
steely glare. She said nothing.

"I'm sorry about not saying good-bye this morning. I had an early
handball game." Still, Wynona spoke no words, but if her look could
have been translated, this story would need an adults-only rating.
Wynona attempted to push her way past Sean, and he stepped in
front of her again.

"I told you I had an early game, and you looked so peaceful sleeping that I didn't want to wake you up." Sean was hoping to find just a
little conciliation in Wynona, but she wasn't budging.

Wynona made one step toward Sean, never breaking her stare,
and finally spoke slowly, clearly, and with great intensity. "I only asked
you to do one thing…one thing. I asked you not to leave without saying good-bye. Was that so difficult for you to do?"

"*Sorry*…what the hell is wrong with you…do you have separation
anxiety or something?" Sean spoke with mocking sincerity because
he was not at all interested in any underlying reason for Wynona's
request. It was enough for him that the request was inconvenient
and therefore was unheeded. At this, Wynona pushed past him with
a forearm to his ribcage that if delivered slightly harder, would have
knocked the air out of his lungs.

"Wynona, come on. Get over it." She walked a few more paces, then stopped as if remembering something. Turning, she slowly walked back to him as he stood unmoving in the hallway. Sean tensed up, not knowing if she was preparing to deliver another blow but this time harder. Wynona came within two feet of Sean, reached into the inner pocket of her jacket, and pulled out a blue toothbrush.

"Here's me getting over it." She then handed him both his tooth-brush and an icy smile.

"Thanks. See, you do care. It's my favorite." With that, he popped it into his mouth and gave Wynona a big grin. "Still tastes minty fresh," he said as he swished it about. Sean was just about to give her a hug when she spun on her heels and was off down the hallway.

"How about dinner tonight?" But without another word, Wynona turned the corner and was gone.

As an associate account representative, Wynona was awarded a cross between a cubicle and an office, or as it was affectionately referred to, a "cubice." Someone else came up with the alternative term "officle," but that never stuck for some reason. The cubice was larger than a traditional cube but did not have a door that needed to be reconfigured if Mr. Smyth had another of his cutting-edge ideas regarding work environment. She entered her cubice like a runner finishing a marathon, threw her bag and notebook on the desk, and opened her computer. Her work area was clean and uncluttered to the point of being Spartan. She had no pictures, knickknacks, or personal memorabilia anywhere within sight. In fact, if not for the name plaque on the wall, one would have thought this was unin-habited office space. Wynona did not believe in the public display of her achievements, nor did she believe in having pictures of family or friends strewn about. The only items allowed were those neces-sary to do her work. She liked to keep her work area simple, focused, and clean—just like she liked to keep her life. Life for Wynona was about order, and anything or anyone that didn't adhere to her strict interpretation of life was either beaten into submission or abandoned to their own chaotic choices.

Wynona did not have many friends. The simple fact was Wynona was not very well liked. She was feared, even respected, but not liked. This was because Wynona didn't like herself very much either. She really hadn't planned on being a bitch, but that was what one became when one was unhappy most of the time. Wynona would have liked to be at peace with herself and others, but somehow she was always in a competition—although competition might be too mild a word, because what Wynona was experiencing was war. A battle raged within her, and the collateral damage created brokenness in her life as well as in the life of every other person she came in contact with. She was not mean; she was wounded and lived out of the pain of those wounds. There were brief times when the pain was less intense and another Wynona peeked out from behind the clouds of suffering, but then she would disappear again, causing those around her to wonder who the true Wynona really was. In reality, Wynona didn't even know who the true Wynona was, and therefore she lived from day to day hoping that somehow, someway, things would get better. But as in a physical injury, the pain doesn't abate until the wound is cleansed and disinfected. Unfortunately, this process often produces the greatest pain.

She pulled up her e-mail messages and saw that within the last hour, she had received three e-mails from her mother—all of which were flagged as urgent. Hesitantly, she picked up her phone and noticed that there were also an equal number of voicemail messages. Taking a glance at her schedule, she came to the painful conclusion that the optimal time to talk to her mother would be right then, so she deleted both the e-mail and voicemail messages without opening them and slowly dialed her mother while bracing herself for another painful conversation with someone she considered certifiably insane.

What then transpired was so out of character for Wynona that it would have been impossible to predict. Wynona started the conversation with her mother as she always did—a combination of insincere words of affection and vocal prompts all designed to give her mother the opportunity to create a controlled release of her emotional reservoir before the dam burst. Typically during one of these conversations, Wynona would be busy working at her computer, but this time, after a few moments, their conversation took an uncharacteristic turn. Wynona stopped multitasking, sat up in her chair, and gave her mother her undivided attention. Her face became ashen as she propped her elbows on her desk, held her head, and spoke in soft, hushed tones. This lasted about fifteen minutes, with Wynona asking several questions and listening intently to each reply. She then hung up the phone, put it in her bag, packed up her laptop, and walked briskly to Mr. Smyth's office.

2
Old Man Stealy

A POLICE CAR turned off the paved county highway, headed up a small dirt road, and after a few twists and turns, traversed a small creek and came within sight of a dilapidated, single-story house almost completely obscured by overgrowth. Parked about a hundred yards from this house was an animal control truck that the squad car passed while continuing on. It finally halted next to a narrow brick path that led to the house's front door. The door of the patrol car opened and out stepped Sheriff Joe Reilly. He was a tall, angular man with a no-nonsense look about him that was in perfect alignment with his personality. Sitting inside the truck were two animal control men. When they saw the police car, they exited their vehicle and walked the final distance to where Sheriff Joe's car was parked. One was a large bald man in his early thirties, who was sweating profusely. An enormous stomach swelled beneath his uniform, which was tenuously held together by two buttons hanging on for dear life. His name was Steve, and in another context, Steve might have been thought of as jolly. But at this place and time, he was more of a jiggling mass of nervous energy. The other man was small and slender with a large mane of bushy, unkempt red hair. His name was Henry, and he quietly trailed behind Steve, who was nervously watching the house as if an attack was imminent. They approached the front of the house where

Sheriff Joe was standing, Henry being very careful to walk directly behind the larger Steve. The house they were approaching was the home of a mysterious recluse named Arnold Stealy, but he had been known in the town as Old Man Stealy for as long as anyone could remember. Some said that he had strange powers and that there were "weird happenings" in his secluded house. Everyone knew he had a love for animals, and rumor had it that they would magically appear from the forest and come to his house to obey his every command. If ignorance were a disease, then the whole town of Brandstad was infected with it regarding Arnold Stealy. They avoided all contact with him, even when he made his rare appearance in town to buy supplies. It was unclear whether it was because of this shunning or because he had a tendency toward paranoia, but Arnold Stealy retreated further and further into his own world and closed off all communication with the town's people. This exacerbated the distance between him and the townspeople further so that he became the probable cause for anything strange, mysterious, or unexplained in the area. Finally, he became the ultimate test for teenage boys eager to prove their manhood. They would sneak into Old Man Stealy's house, take something, and then return to their friends with a trophy to prove their bravery. It was after one of these adventures that word got out that he had a large number of animals on his property, and pressure was put on the county animal control authorities to investigate, which Arnold Stealy did not allow.

Steve and Henry approached Sheriff Joe, who was peering at the house. "Couldn't get any closer, huh?" Sheriff Joe mumbled as he lit his cigarette.

"You know it's not safe. Remember what happened last week?" Steve pointed at a chunk that was missing from the small white fence where Stealy's shotgun blast had landed. "He could have killed us."

"If he had wanted to kill you, you'd be dead. I've known Old Man Stealy for fifty years, and he's not about to hurt anyone unless they mean to hurt him or one of his animals."

"Just the same, I'm glad you're here, Sheriff, because we can't do our job unless you protect us from..."

Sheriff Joe was clearly annoyed with the task he was required to perform and just walked away in disgust while Steve was talking. "Hell, I'm only here because his daughter in California is worried. She hasn't heard from him in a few days, and he isn't answering his phone."

Steve took Sheriff Joe's cue and began to walk toward the house with Henry still trailing behind him, obviously using him as a human shield. "But you've got to help us if there's any problem. If he's in violation of county animal codes by keeping illegal animals, then we've got to remove those animals."

Henry was usually content with quietly supporting Steve, but he now felt compelled to echo his partner's concern. "From the description we got, we think some of the animals are on the endangered species list. So if we need to remove these animals, you're gonna make sure there's no shooting...right?" Henry and Steve's number-one priority was for their own personal safety; animal welfare came in a very distant third behind getting back in time for lunch.

Sheriff Joe turned abruptly around and surveyed the two scared county workers. "Where you from, boys?"

Steve responded with some smugness, "Seattle." Henry nodded his head in agreement.

"Well, in this town, we do things a little different. We don't mess with someone unless they're a danger to themselves or others. We believe in the First Amendment."

"Isn't the First Amendment freedom of speech?" Steve didn't mean to correct the sheriff with his question. But he did, and it only further irritated the sheriff.

"I mean whatever damned amendment keeps people like you out of other people's business. Got it?" The sheriff was in no mood to have his constitutional knowledge questioned.

"But the county code..." Henry whined.

Sheriff Joe took a long drag from his cigarette and blew a cloud of smoke in their faces. "If you do anything to upset this man, I will personally take your codebook and shove it so far up your butts that you'll need to stick out your tongue to read it. Do you get my meaning, boys?" Not waiting for an answer, Sheriff Joe walked up to the porch and prepared to knock on the door but then thought better of it. He stepped back and called out.

"Hey, Mr. Stealy, it's Sheriff Joe. We're just checking to see if you're OK." He paused for a moment to see if there was an answer, but there was nothing to be heard but the occasional bark of a dog.

"Mr. Stealy, we've got to check on you because your daughter, Miley, is worried. Can you hear me?" Again there was no answer, so Sheriff Joe turned the doorknob and pushed. It was open.

"Bet it's a trap," Henry muttered.

Sheriff Joe continued to knock on the door as he stepped into the house. "Mr. Stealy, it's Sheriff Joe. I'm coming in, and all I want to know is if you're OK, so don't do anything foolish." He stepped into the living room, which was cluttered with years of books, magazines, and other stuff that may have at one time been useful but now was just junk. There was an old shell of a stand-up radio in the corner next to a half-finished wicker chair and piles of *National Geographic* issues. In another corner, there were piles of plastic bags and stacks of newspapers. Sheriff Joe thought to himself, *It would be easy to lose someone in here.*

"Get in here, you wusses, and help me find him." The twosome, still standing in the doorway, made hesitant steps into the room.

"You guys check in here and the kitchen, and I'll go look in the bedrooms." Sheriff Joe pushed past the clutter and headed toward what he hoped was the back of the house. He found a path that wound its way around large piles of books and loose papers and came to what looked to be a bedroom door. Up to then, he had not seen even one animal, which was surprising since he had also heard the rumors about how Old Man Stealy kept hundreds of pets and exotic animals.

The door was already ajar, so he pushed it open and looked into the dimly lit room. There, against the headboard, propped up by pillows, was Old Man Stealy—obviously deceased. Looking about the room, Sheriff Joe knew where all the animals had gone. They encircled Mr. Stealy like he was giving a performance onstage. There were dozens of cats, and interspersed among them were marmots, weasels, skunks, and a few very large ratlike creatures as well as something that looked like a porcupine. This was a very strange sight, but the strangest part was they were all focused entirely on Arnold Stealy as if he were lecturing them on some important topic. They didn't even break their concentration when Sheriff Joe entered the room. Not one head turned from the object of their attention.

"I found him," shouted Sheriff Joe as he stepped farther into the room and tried to apprehend the macabre situation.

The two animal control officers pushed their way through mounds of trash and peered into the room.

"What a sight," Henry exclaimed in a hushed, reverent voice.

"Yeah, you don't see this every day," responded Steve. "There must be at least a dozen species in here."

Sheriff Joe gave the two an incredulous look and shook his head at the inane comment. "I guess you boys will be wanting to cage these animals."

"Eventually," replied Steve, who was now feeling a bit relieved that all he needed to deal with was animals and not Mr. Stealy. "But first, we need to have a look around because we think there may be bigger fish on this property. Not that we're looking for fish, you know, but...It's a metaphor, you know..." Steve withered under the glare of the sheriff and actually forgot what he was saying while he was speaking.

"Get to it. I've got to call this in." Sheriff Joe pushed past the two men, who were still marveling at the assortment of assembled animals. He followed the path back to the front door and walked to his patrol car to tell his dispatcher to send for the coroner, and then he

heard a shout come from behind the house. He put down the microphone and found a narrow pebble path leading around the house,
where he came upon Steve and Henry. There in the back was a series
of enclosures. He joined the other two men and found a cement walkway that bisected at least fifty enclosures on either side. Some of
the cages were small pens, but some were capable of keeping larger
animals. On the door of each enclosure was a chart that gave the animal's name, history, and information on the specific care.

"He had himself a regular zoo," Henry said.

As they proceeded down the walkway, they passed a cage holding a mountain lion with a bandaged leg next to an enclosure with a
mountain goat. The facility held dozens of animals in various states
of medical care, but all seemed in fairly good condition. Finally, they
came to the last and largest of the enclosures. This one was open
and empty. There was no chart on the door, and the only indication
something was supposed to be in it was a hand-drawn sign that read,
"Dragon. Beware!"

Henry read the sign out loud and gasped. "What the heck did he
keep in here?"

Sheriff Joe looked into the enclosure and then noticed a large
set of very unusual tracks originating from the enclosure and leading
out of the compound into the surrounding forest. He peered out to
the place in the dense woods where the tracks disappeared and muttered to himself, "And where the hell did it go?"

3
LARPs

THE WOODS WERE cool, with a morning mist hanging over a long and narrow meadow that made a gap between stands of birch trees. The sunlight had not yet risen past the tree line, and long shadows stretched from one side to the other. This part of the forest was made up of gently rolling terrain highlighted by several rocky hills that had been formed by the process of ancient glaciers slowly grinding the earth, which gave this area a unique topography. It was midsummer, and the flowers of the season had pushed their way up through the grasses and created a stunning, multicolored carpet. Winter was harsh in these woods, and spring often didn't yield its promised warmth, so when the southerly wind finally brought its awakening caresses, it was welcomed wholeheartedly by all who lived in the forest as well as those who visited. The meadow could only be accessed by a narrow trail that wound its way around several elevated rock outcroppings and then down into an indent in the terrain that followed a small but lively stream. It was from one of these high places that a band of four unusual travelers moved quickly along the shadowy path.

"We've only about a mile to go," said the tall young man in the lead. He was clothed in buckskin lined with fur that accentuated his athletic physique. He wore knee-length leather boots and a metal helmet that was obviously hand forged. He was muscular and fair, with long blond hair that trailed behind him like a horse's mane. Strapped to his back was a scabbard holding a long and dangerous-looking sword.

"Wait...Hold up. I've got to fix my belt." Just then, a short young man came around the corner and broke into a patch of sunlight on the path. He was garbed in what could only be described as medieval chain mail that reached all the way to his shins. The mail was cinched at the waist by a wide leather belt that held an assortment of pouches and tools, one of which was a large battle ax. Slung over his shoulder was an ox horn encrusted with a silver emblem. It was clear he was having a wardrobe malfunction because his belt had slid down past his waist and was threatening to foul his feet, which would have pitched him on his face. But currently it merely reduced his walking to a slow waddle.

The tall, fair-haired young man did not stop but motioned with his hands in disgust. "Kyle, can't you get it together, just once!"

Just then, an elflike woman came up to the distressed little man. She was slender and wore a diaphanous dress that flowed with emerald greens and turquoise blues. Her long, blond, braided hair was dotted with baby's breath and about her neck was a golden chain with a delicate silver design of a unicorn dancing. Across her back was a quiver of handmade arrows, and she carried a bow that was also not commercially fashioned. She stretched out her hand and placed it upon the little man's face. "His name is not Kyle. It is Brummel the Dwarf. We are on an adventure, and when we are on an adventure, his name is Brummel the Dwarf just like you are the warrior, Perales the Proud. And we're not in such a hurry that we can't give him some time to pull up his pants."

At this, the tall young man stopped and turned around and spoke in a more pleading tone. "You know we lose experience points if we're late."

Then, from the shadows stepped an equally tall man, clothed from head to foot in a dark-brown hooded robe made of a heavy woven fabric and cinched at the waist with a wide hemp rope knotted at the ends. He was called Wanderer, and he was the wizard of the little band. His hood obscured his face so that when he spoke, it was as if the sound were coming from somewhere deep in the recesses of his robe. The only other parts of his wardrobe were leather sandals and a long, sturdy staff.

"Alliea is right. We have time," came a deep voice from the robed man.

The dwarf quickly refastened his belt, adjusted his assortment of gear, and walked on with a more normal stride. The group's destination was a steeper part of the meadow where the stream was bisected by a small wooden bridge. There they were to meet the Mysterions of Glenbrook in mortal combat.

They were silently following the path that now trailed the stream, when the hooded man began to hum. His humming gradually became louder, with the others joining in. The music had a Celtic feel to it and seemed perfectly suited to the cadence of their walk. They eventually all joined in, softly singing these words:

> From ancient times we come
> To seek our quest and fate.
> To danger we will run.
> All cowards we will hate.
> And now the quest begun
> To prove ourselves as great
> With the rising of the sun,
> With the rising of the sun.

Gradually the song increased both in volume and intensity until the last line of the chorus almost became a shout. Eventually, this strange little band ended up on the high side of one of the slopes that created a U-shaped valley with the small stream below spanned by a small footbridge. There they stood and waited in silence while looking across the valley. It was then that a figure appeared from the lower end of the valley and walked slowly up to the bridge. The figure was hooded, dressed in a long purple robe, like one might see in a Shakespearean play, and he carried a large sack. He placed himself on one side of the stream, next to the bridge. Then, on the opposite side of the slope, a group of four similarly dressed individuals appeared and stood silently across the valley. The man in the purple robe began to unpack his sack and walk around the area, placing objects in various locations. He then drew out a small chair and a horn, similar to the one Brummel was carrying but less elaborate. He blew the horn once, and the two groups began shouting at the top of their lungs. He blew it again, and they both made a mad dash to where the purple-robed man was sitting.

The two parties arrived almost simultaneously and were equally out of breath. The robed man stood up, and a hush fell on the gathering.

"We are here to test will and skill, heart and valor, and the strength of your fellowship. Those who triumph will be well rewarded; those who are vanquished will grow in humility." He then turned to the groups on either side of the stream. "Mysterions, are you ready?" There was a loud shout from this group. Then he turned to the first group and looked down at a small notebook.

"Hemorrhoids, are you ready?"

Uncontrollable laughter broke out from the Mysterions. Perales blushed with anger and shouted. "Whoa, mister game ref, I don't think that's the way it's supposed to be said!"

Alliea punched Perales in the side and scolded, "I told you it wouldn't work, but no, you had to have the name of a Greek god."

"Damn right. Only a Greek god is good enough for me."

Wanderer stepped forward and spoke slowly and with perfect diction: "Excuse me, your honor, but the name of our fellowship is Hermetoids. Named after Hermes, the ancient Greek messenger god and protector of those most vulnerable. If it pleases you, we are ready to commence the contest."

The Hermetoids were fairly new to the world of live action role playing, or LARP, and had only recently founded their fellowship. It was not that they were new to the world of gaming, for most had been avid gamers since they were classmates in high school, but they had become bored with the lack of personal involvement and longed to immerse themselves, body and soul, in the world in which their characters lived. It was Kyle (Brummel) who first had attended a LARP convention and then sought out the local LARP organization near their town. Kyle was not very social and didn't have many friends, so he decided to put an ad in the weekly *Gazette* to see if he'd get any takers. That is how this unlikely group of individuals had found one another.

Becoming a LARPer is no easy process, especially the kind of LARPers that were in this particular region. LARPing was not a game to these individuals; it was a way of life. They incarnated their characters, and in a strange, almost mystical way, their characters gave birth to them. Their clothes were meticulously created, with every fiber and every stitch made to be as authentic as possible. In the world of LARPers, there were no sewing machines or synthetic fabrics, so every item had to be handmade, handwoven, and absolutely true to its history. Each LARP character had an extensive backstory that came into play and expanded with each adventure. Players were expected to act according to their creeds and to prize fidelity to their fellowships above all other virtues. In a world where it seemed that people cared less and less about each other and where isolation seemed more the norm than the exception, becoming a LARP touched the deep recesses of their souls as no other hobby could.

This was only their second contest, and the first under their new name. The official in the purple robe was known as the high master of the contest (MOC), and it was his duty to preside over the contest. The contests were designed to test each character's skill in their craft. For example, a wizard would be required to know spells and the ancient lore from which they sprung. Wizards were also tested for wisdom and the ability to work through difficult and perplexing problems. They were often read ancient riddles by the MOC and asked to formulate a solution. These conundrums, though difficult, required more than just a quick intellect; they required a wise heart and a just spirit. Wanderer had already gained some approving nods from the MOC over the creative and ingenious way he solved the "Battle of the Brother Elves," which was a story that the MOC pulled out for rookies to humble them. The story was about two elves who were fighting over the love of a princess, and the wizard must decide which brother was most worthy of her hand in marriage. Most wizards focused upon the elves' accomplishments and external attributes, but Wanderer went right to the heart of the issue and focused upon which of the two had true love. This true love was determined, in the words of Wanderer, not by how much the brother loved, but by how much the brother was loved; for true love always came from a true heart, and that heart would show itself in every relationship. The MOC had been very impressed.

Those who had chosen elf as their character would be tested in their agility in the use of bow and arrow, as well as their knowledge of flora and fauna. Alliea was not the best suited for the woodland craft aspect of being an elf. When she was in Girl Scouts, she caused a small forest fire when she sneaked out of camp to smoke a joint with a few other delinquents. However, Alliea had a newly acquired love for the forest since becoming a LARPer and was developing an appreciation for the richness of nature's beauty, especially when she began to see it through the eyes of Wanderer.

Dwarves might be asked to throw their war ax at a target or give a recitation on geology or on methods of forging and shaping metal. Brummel, like the rest, was extremely new to LARPing, and he had not completely mastered the art of being a dwarf, but he was a dwarf at heart and in spirit. Dwarves are extremely focused creatures; when they set upon a task or project, they always see it through, no matter how hard it is or how long it takes. Brummel may have been unable to wield a war ax well, but he was diligent to learn all the dwarf lore down to the first generation. It was probably his years of isolation as a child—and now into his young adulthood—that had honed his focus and made him dwarflike.

The warrior was expected to be both strong and skillful in the use of several weapons. He was also tested on his courage and self-sacrificing nature, and this was often a very difficult test. Perales, also known as Connor Reilly, was, like the rest, new to the LARP experience and derived his motivation more from the football field than from fantasy literature. He therefore preferred trash talking his opponent and taking every opportunity to dis the opposition. This did not go over well with the MOC and gave their fellowship a poor reputation among the other LARPers. In the world of LARPing, when insulting the other fellowship, it was very important that it be done skillfully and cleverly and be nuanced in such a way that those being insulted were not certain they had been insulted. This Perales could not do, especially when he was angry, which was almost all the time, so his insults sounded like the idiotic cursing of a dull-witted moron. When he went off on one of his tirades, the MOC would grimace, shake his head, and immediately lower his score.

Much depended on the judgment of the MOC, so his identity was always disguised by a mask for fear that some would exert undue influence upon him between campaigns. He not only oversaw the objective aspects of the contest, as in archery or questions about forest herbs, but he also looked deeper into the hearts of the characters to see if they had developed the true soul of a LARPer. These tests were often the most difficult and left the LARPers with a sense of reverence and fear as they began each contest. To this end, the MOC developed tests for the teams that required that they work together and resolve any conflict with the good of the fellowship in mind.

All was prepared, and the contest commenced. But to say it was a contest would be to make too much of the effort of the Hermetoids, for they were greatly outmatched. Perales was first up, and the MOC ordered that a long, narrow board be stretched between the two banks of the stream. This could mean only one thing—they would be required to "Little John." The warriors on both teams were given staffs with large leather-padded ends and were required to advance onto the plank from opposite ends. When they met in the middle, they would attempt to put each other into the stream using the padded end of their staffs; hence the name given to this contest, from the famous bout between Robin Hood and his soon-to-be friend, Little John. Perales was strong, but it took a great deal more than strength to win this contest. In fact, if the warrior was skilled, he would use the strength of his opponent against him. Perales approached his opponent with self-assurance and strode to the middle of the stream, raised his staff, and took one large, uncontrolled swipe. The Mysterion warrior easily avoided Perales's attack and waited patiently until Perales's backswing caused him to become unstable. It was then just a matter of a small nudge, and Perales fell headlong into the ice-cold stream with practically no effort expended on the part of the other warrior. The Hermetoids looked away to spare the feelings of the humiliated Perales as he sloshed his way to the edge of the stream, stumbled up the slippery bank, and joined his fellowship.

There were a few moments when the Hermetoids showed some ability, such as when Wanderer presented a complete forty-stanza rendition of his ancestors and their glorious achievements. Or when Alliea was challenged to a duel of nimbleness. Her opponent showed her adeptness by walking on her hands for about twenty feet and then rolled out into a perfect somersault. Alliea gave a confident smile, took off her quiver, handed it to Perales, gave a wink to the master of the contest, and then leaped up on the railing of the foot-bridge and treated it as if it were a gymnastics balance beam. With a combination of handstands and twists, she was magnificent. But unfortunately, when asked by the MOC to identify tree leaves, she could not tell an oak from a maple, which is very un-elf-like, and caused her to lose her contest. The match seemed all but over, with the Mysterions having the overwhelming advantage, when Brummel called for a time-out.

The Hermetoids assembled just out of earshot of the other group, and Brummel said in a hushed whisper, "We are losing this for sure."

"No thanks to you. You were supposed to study your metals!" Alliea snorted.

Perales interrupted, "Let's not talk about knowing things...like the difference between a freaking oak and a maple!"

Alliea turned to Perales, who was standing next to her. "You're dripping on me."

Wanderer put up his hand, and the others grew silent. "We can all see that we are losing, and there is no shame in it if we have done our best. So why did you call this council"

Brummel spoke hesitantly because he was not comfortable with expressing his thoughts. "We could turn this around in our favor with one blow of the horn of destiny." As he spoke, the dwarf removed the horn that was slung on his shoulder and held it out for the others to see.

Brummel had come into possession of the Horn of Power while attending a national LARP convention in a large city several hours' drive from Brandstad. This was when Brummel, then known as Kyle, was just stepping into the world of LARPing, and before the forma-tion of the Hermetoid fellowship. Kyle was alone, as he was most of the time, and walking around the large convention center visiting numerous tables and booths set up throughout. Kyle was beginning his investigation of the world of LARPing, as did many, with the hope

of finding himself through creating an alternate persona and inhab-
iting its world. It was the last day of the convention, and, preparing
for the long drive home, Kyle wandered into a corner of the convention center where he thought he might find the men's room. It was
there that he stumbled upon an elderly man in a perfectly appointed
dwarf outfit, sitting behind a table in front of an ornate display of
dwarf artistry. His long, unkempt hair poured like a white waterfall
from underneath his wool cap, cascading to his broad shoulders.
Kyle could not see his eyes, partly because his head was bowed
and partly because of his bushy white eyebrows, which seemed to
sprout wildly in all directions over his eyes. His nose was enormous
and pockmarked and looked altogether like a cheese grater. The old
dwarf was sitting quietly with his head bowed so that his long white
beard hid his hands, which were folded upon his lap. Kyle had not yet
decided upon his LARP character, but during the conference, he had
been strangely drawn to the dwarves. This may have been because
of his smallish stature, but it was more likely because they seemed
to be the most serious and detail-oriented of the characters. He
walked up to the man behind the table, intending to ask directions
to the restroom, but he appeared to be asleep so he continued past
the table. Suddenly he heard a voice call out, "Hail, fellow dwarf."
Kyle turned to see where the voice had come from but saw no one
except for the ancient dwarf who was fast asleep. He stopped for a
moment and waited to see if anyone spoke again, and when no one
did, he turned and began to walk away. But the voice repeated, "Hail,
fellow dwarf."

This time he was certain it was coming from the old dwarf, so he
took a step toward the table and said sheepishly, "You mean me?"

The old man lifted his head, and Kyle could immediately see
that he was blind. "Yes, of course I mean you. Do you see any other
dwarves about?"

Kyle stammered a bit and finally said, "I'm not really a LARP yet,
and I'm not sure what I will be if and when I become one."

"Of course you're a dwarf. I can feel it. But what is more important is that *you* can feel it. I should know. I have been campaigning since before you were born. Let me ask you—have you chosen your token yet?"

"Token?"

"Yes, the sacred item you will treasure as you go into your campaigns."

"I have not been on any campaigns. I don't even have a fellowship, so, no, I don't have a token."

The old man rose and went into a small enclosure behind him while Kyle stood watching. "Well, what are you waiting for? Come with me." The old dwarf spoke gruffly but not unkindly. And, completely out of character for Kyle, he followed the old dwarf into the tent. He saw dozens of beautiful, intricately made objects hanging on the walls. There were bronze war axes, elaborately carved breastplates that looked to be inlaid with gold, and helmets edged with copper and encrusted with jewels.

"Sit." The old dwarf pointed to a wooden stool that faced the assortment of objects on the wall, and Kyle obediently sat. The old dwarf then took a piece of cloth and wrapped it around Kyle's eyes so that he couldn't see. "Put out your hands with your palms up and then repeat after me."

I follow the ancient way
Of rock and stone and mountain.
Deep within the earth I came
From the eternal fountain.
I will revere the way of the dwarf
And bring honor to my clan.
With this token, I make my pledge
As it is placed into my hand.

When Kyle said these last words, the old dwarf placed an ivory object into his hands and then took off Kyle's blindfold. It was then that Kyle looked with astonishment at the Horn of Power for the first time.

"This is your token as you enter the fellowship of the dwarves." The old dwarf then picked up a scroll and gave it to Kyle. "This will tell you what you need to know about the Horn of Power."

Kyle was still staring at the object in his hands when he suddenly remembered he was at a convention and all the booths were there to sell their wares, not give them away. "I can't afford anything like this."

The old dwarf was now exiting the tent. "Did I ask you for money?"

"No, but..."

The old dwarf turned to look at Kyle with unseeing eyes, and Kyle felt he saw him more completely than anyone had ever seen him before. "Brummel, I do not sell tokens. They are always given."

"Brummel? Who's he?" Kyle began to be concerned that he was not dealing with someone who was completely sane.

"Brummel is your name, and you are now from the clan of the western mountain dwarves. It is a very old and very noble clan. You now have a family, and it is your duty to bring honor to your clan." Kyle felt like he was in a dream. He was completely unaccustomed to being invited to be a part of anything, much less an ancient clan of dwarves. All he could do was say thank you because he was overcome by emotion.

The old dwarf handed Kyle a small parchment card. "Here is where I can be reached. You will receive information about clan meetings. Look for it. Now, go find your fellowship, and bring honor to the dwarf nation." The old dwarf then sat down at his table, bowed his head and took the same position as when Kyle had first seen him. Kyle was about to leave, but then he had an overpowering urge to ask one more question.

"Sir, how did you choose this as my token out of all those that were on the wall?"

The old dwarf did not raise his head but spoke in a voice both clear and powerful. "A dwarf does not choose his token. The token chooses the dwarf. You were made for the Horn of Power, and the Horn of Power was made for you. Be careful to use it for a noble purpose in a time of great need."

Kyle left without knowing anything more about the old dwarf or even how he would learn more about his new clan. But he knew this was the beginning of his new life as a LARPer.

Now, hoping to save face for the Hermetoids in their contest with the Mysterions, Kyle made a proposal. "You know that I acquired this from an ancient dwarf who took it through many adventures and campaigns. It has never been used and has great power. One blow and it will change our fortunes completely."

Wanderer gently touched the precious possession. "My fellow, you do not know with certainty what will happen when you blow this horn. For it can be blown only once, and then only in the most desperate need. Has that time now come?"

Brummel looked at Wanderer and then the rest of the company. "Why carry it around if we don't use it?"

"I say use it now." Perales stepped into the circle and grabbed the horn and began to put it to his lips. Then with one swift poke to the abdomen with his staff, Wanderer caused the horn to pop out of Perales's hands.

"You cannot use it. If you try, it will render it useless. It can be used only by Brummel. It is dwarf-made, and only a dwarf has the right to summon Its power." Wanderer stood face to face with Perales, who was seething with anger at being made to look foolish.

After regaining his breath, Perales attempted to regain some dignity. "So you say, Wizard, but how do we know you're right?"

Brummel spoke up. "He's right. That is what I was told, and the horn came with a scroll." He reached into one of his bags, unraveled a scroll, and read,

In a time of dread and woe,
Hope is lost and darkness grows.
Hear these words, and you will know
A miracle happens with one blow.

"So if this is not that day, when is?" the little dwarf asked beseechingly.

"Search your heart, Brummel. Have you lost all hope and does darkness indeed grow? Even if we lose this contest, is that worthy of a miracle?" He put his hand on the dwarf's shoulder, and the dwarf slowly nodded his head. "Save it for another day, a day when you will know to use it with certainty."

With that, the Hermetoids finished their council and, as they fully expected, lost the contest. They were sent home to develop their skills and grow in humility, a lesson that some in their fellowship resisted.

4
Wynona Leaves the City

WYNONA APPROACHED MR. Smyth's office, walked in without knocking, closed the door behind her, and had a conversation that lasted about five minutes. She then walked out of his office and straight for the elevators without a word of explanation.

Her time at her apartment was almost as brief as her time at the office. She packed a small duffel bag, threw her travel toiletries into it, grabbed her car keys, locked the door, and she was gone. Within one hour, Wynona's entire schedule was thrown away, and there was only one thought on her mind, one priority on her agenda—going home.

If anyone had told Wynona the day before that she would be voluntarily driving the eight hundred miles home, she would have said they were cracked. But here she was on a long-distance drive to a place that she loathed. Home had no pleasant memories for Wynona. So what was it that could change the course of her life with a phone call? In one word—Beth. Beth was Wynona's older sister by three years, and she was the only person on earth who she truly cared for. Beth and Wynona had formed an unbreakable bond, not just because they were sisters, but because they were sisters who truly loved each other. This bond was perhaps because of the tragic death of their father when Wynona was six, or possibly it was because of the completely insane way their mother, June, had raised them after their father had died. It's been said that those who go through a traumatic experience together often develop a lifelong bond. Wynona and Beth's bond was forged through the trauma of losing a loving father, but it was tempered in the fire of living with June, a woman who was as hard to live with as a house full of biting fleas.

But probably the greatest reason for the love Wynona had for Beth was that Beth was the only one that she truly trusted. The reason for this was that Beth loved Wynona with a strong, secure, and enduring love that would not shrink back in the face of one of Wynona's selfish tirades or childish episodes. Beth was what she called a "sticker." She would not be shaken off, thrown off, or ignored. Her love for Wynona saw right through the shatterproof exterior Wynona showed to the rest of the world. To Beth, Wynona would always be that inconsolable little girl who heard that the most important person in her life was never coming home. So when Beth spoke to Wynona, she always spoke to this part of her. When Beth needed to forgive Wynona, it was because she could forgive this hurting part of her that was hurting others. And this was what made Wynona feel safe, truly safe, with Beth. She knew that she didn't have to do anything, be anything, or say anything to make Beth love her, because she had said all the most hurtful things one could say to another, and Beth's love stuck.

But now she had news that put everything in her world into the spin cycle of confusion and despair. The phone call from her mother had not been just another annoying guilt-ridden tête-à-tête. Her mother had given her the news that the one person she had counted on to always be there had been diagnosed with terminal cancer and given only weeks to live. *How can this be? What God in the universe would take the life of the only truly good person I know?* These questions and more were racing through Wynona's mind while she didn't stop for anything but gas and exceeded all speed limits.

Ahead was a sign: "Brandstad, 60 miles." Wynona took a deep breath and began to prepare herself for the flaming reentry into an atmosphere that she had escaped six years ago and vowed never to enter again. Brandstad started as a logging community and was especially prone to fires due to the combination of its heavily forested surroundings and the south winds that would occasionally blow in the driest part of summer. During these times, it took only one spark to send the town into a fiery oblivion. So in the last century, when the small logging community had had an especially bad run-in with the flames, someone had the bright idea to name the town Brandstad, which was Swedish for "fire town."

It was shortly after midnight when Wynona drove down Main Street and parked in front of Bill's Diner. She had driven for about twelve hours straight and needed to unwind before she entered the unknown world of Beth's illness. Bill's Diner was always open due to the truck and interstate traffic that came through the city. Unlike most cities that had been bypassed by the modern interstate system, Brandstad was one of those rare towns that remained a place that travelers needed to pass through to get from here to there. And because of that, there was always someone at Bill's.

Wynona turned off her car and sat for a moment. She had forgotten how quiet Brandstad was. *Yes, quiet like a grave*, she thought as she stepped out of her car. The lights from Bill's splashed across the sidewalk, and the neon sign above the door gave an eerie radiance to those who entered. Nothing had changed in the six years since Wynona had been home. The counter was right out of a fifties diner, which made sense because that was the last time Bill had remodeled. She found a booth in the corner, against the wall, and hoped she would avoid seeing anyone she knew. Wynona quickly buried herself behind the menu, which also hadn't changed.

"Wynona, darling, is that you?" Clara, the ageless, timeless, and to Wynona's mind, clueless waitress, came rushing over and jerked her up out of her seat. "Let me look at you, doll. Yep, you're all grown up and looking mighty citified." Ever since Clara had babysat for Wynona and Beth, she felt she had the right to call them baby names. It never bothered Beth, but it irritated the hell out of Wynona. Then Clara's voice got low and a look of intense sadness came over her. "And I know why you're here. Oh, baby, I'm so sorry about Beth. We're all just so sad about—"

At this, Wynona somehow extricated herself from the clasp of the well-meaning Clara and tried to redirect what was about to become an unwelcome conversation.

"Yes, well, Clara, it is good to see you too, and I look forward to a longer visit, but just now, do you suppose I could get some of your good coffee, and what have you got for soup today?"

Clara looked empathically at Wynona and then gave her a wink. "OK, baby, you have it your way…You always do. Let me get you some of our good beef barley and a cup of hot coffee."

Clara shuffled off to the kitchen, leaving Wynona to scan the room for other possible dangerous people. At the other end of the diner, she saw a trio of former high school classmates who seemed so intensely into their own conversation that they hadn't noticed Clara's announcing to the world that she was home. She vaguely remembered two of them and searched her memory to place them in their respective groups. All high schools have groups: there are the jocks, the nerds, the arts freaks, the druggies, and so forth. Wynona fell into a very small group of invisibles who hated school and hated the cliques and who just wanted out as fast as possible. But she did notice that of the three at the table, one was a member of the jocks and was, in fact, the captain of the football team. His name was Connor Reilly, the hapless son of Sheriff Joe Reilly. The other girl that Wynona recognized was Lori Summerville, and her group had been a clique of one. She was the privileged elite of Brandstad High School because her father owned the logging company, which was the largest business in town. This honor ensured that everyone in school sucked up to her…even the teachers. The last one at the table was a small fat guy who vaguely looked like someone she used to see hanging out in the science lab. But the eight years had not been kind to him, and he seemed to have put on about fifty pounds. She couldn't remember his name—probably because she never knew it.

Her focus on that group was bringing back a torrent of unwelcome memories, interrupted only when Clara placed a bowl of steaming soup in front of her. "Eat up, hon." Clara poured a large cup of coffee for her and, when done, stopped and stood in front of her with a big goofy grin. This went on for what seemed like an eternity. Wynona finally broke the silence. "What?" she asked impatiently.

"Don't you see?"

Clara was still trying to suppress her excitement.

"Clara, it's been a long, long drive, and I'm really not up for one of your guessing games, so if you have something to say, just say it." Wynona took a sip of her coffee and burned her lips. "Ouch!"

"Careful, dear. The coffee is hot." Again Clara smiled at Wynona, but this time she seemed to be motioning with her body in the direction of the kitchen, which was visible through an open pass behind the counter. Behind where the dishes were placed for the waitresses, she noticed a young man working the grill. At first he was facing away from her, and all she could see was his muscular back outlined perfectly beneath a thin white T-shirt, but when he turned around, she caught a glimpse of his face. Wynona gave an audible gasp. "Oh shit!"

Clara turned back to Wynona with a look of surprise. "Why, child, such language. Is that what you're learning in the big city?"

Wynona recognized the young man as Brandon George, her first and only boyfriend in high school. She'd said good-bye to Brandon when she said good-bye to Brandstad, with a clean, surgical cut. Since then, there had been no communication between them. At first, Brandon sent letters and even attempted to call her a few times, but Wynona fended off all overtures and made sure she never gave him reason to believe there was any chance of them becoming a couple. Brandon epitomized everything that she hated about the small town of Brandstad—small dreams, small ambitions, small minds, small everything.

Clara appeared ready to call out to Brandon when Wynona diverted her attention. "You know, it's late and I'm tired, so why don't we save this reunion for when I'm feeling better."

Clara had already seen that Wynona was acting, as she would say, peevish, so she agreed to this. Clara was a romantic, and she knew that the right moment for a lovers' reunion was essential for the story to end happily ever after.

"OK, sweetie, you eat up and get your strength back. He ain't going anywhere."

And that was exactly what Wynona believed. Brandon was going nowhere, and the perfect evidence of this fact was that he was working as a short-order cook in a greasy spoon in a back-assward town.

Wynona finished her soup and coffee and dropped a ten spot on the table. She slipped out unnoticed by her former classmates. Once outside, she took a deep breath and wondered if it was going to be this hard for the entire time. Then she remembered that the reason she had come was far more excruciating than meeting people from her past. Her sister, Beth, was dying.

5
Arriving Home

BRANDSTAD WAS MADE up of neat homes with steep roofs to shed the heavy snows of winter. Most of the homes were built around the turn of the last century and had been maintained meticulously by their current inhabitants. The lawns were lush, green, and weed-free, as were the attached gardens, which were tended to perfection, evidencing the high value that was placed upon external appearance. The roots of this town were planted firmly in the acidic soil of the Protestant ethic so that even in the worst of times, there would be no outward evidence. Geographically, the town was nestled in a series of small mountains, none of which could claim notability, but in combination, they made for some very lovely scenery. These mountains dotted the surrounding forest as rocky peaks jutting above the tree line, hording the winter snows well into early summer. They fed a few pristine lakes with crystal-clear water. But the beauty of the region was mostly lost on the townspeople, for the region was known for growing good trees for the logging industry, and tree sap was the lifeblood of Brandstad.

Wynona got into her car and drove the short distance to her mother's house. It was almost 1:00 a.m. when she arrived in Brandstad. She had predetermined that she'd not wake anyone and just head for her former bedroom upstairs, which her mother told her would be waiting. Her mother also told her that Beth was in the downstairs den, which had been turned into a bedroom for easier access to the medical equipment that made her life more comfortable. Beth surrounded by a room filled with monitors and machines was not a sight Wynona was eager to see.

Driving the empty streets, she saw old haunts that brought back memories of her childhood years, some good but mostly bad. There was the corner where she got in her first fight with Sally Magden, who said that Wynona was too small to play hide-and-seek. Sally regretted that decision because even though she was two years older and three inches taller, Wynona had knocked her down and sent her running for home. Wynona turned up Elm Street, and there in the Gustafsons' yard was the treehouse that she loved to play in as a kid. It seemed like it was a thousand feet in the air when she was a child. When she was up there, she could see all the way to the train trestle at the edge of town. It was also the place she had her first kiss with Jimmy Gustafson. He was a plump eight-year-old with blond hair and a full set of gleaming braces. But they hadn't been gleaming at that time, because he was right in the middle of a sloppy Tootsie Roll when his amorous compulsion came upon him. She also remembered that he regretted the day because his punishment was being dangled from the trapdoor of his treehouse while screaming for his mommy until he swore he would never do it again. Hearing Jimmy's screams, Mrs. Gustafson came running from the house, hysterical at the sight of her precious Jimmy's precarious predicament. She stood screaming up at Wynona to let her son go, and then thought better of that request and shouted at her not to let him go. This incident may have been when Wynona got her reputation as a troubled child. Shortly thereafter, kids ceased to invite her over to their houses to play and parents made sure she was not on their children's birthday lists. It seemed that most of Wynona's childhood memories were of being on the outside and excluded from the normal people of Brandstad.

But these memories were all put behind her when she exceeded their expectations.

"Well, I won," she said audibly as her car pulled up in front of the white, three-bedroom, one-and-a-half-bath, two-story house she had called home for the first eighteen years of her life. She grabbed her bag and briefcase and opened the gate on the white picket fence. Wynona used to fantasize that white picket fences were secret alien-signaling devices and that the people of Brandstad were really a race from another planet who would someday conquer the earth. It was either that, or creative landscaping simply did not exist in Brandstad. She preferred the extraterrestrial theory.

It was almost a full moon, so there was plenty of light to lead her up to the house and up the four front steps onto the wide front porch. The house had been built in a day when people used to sit on their front porches during the long days of summer and greet their neighbors who were out taking their constitutionals after dinner. She approached the front door, and looked around for the little clay bunny that had always hidden the key. She found it, unlocked the door, and attempted to slip into the house undetected. This was no easy task because this was an old house, and it seemed not to like keeping anyone's movements a secret. With every step Wynona took, there was a creak and then a crack and then a shudder. She recalled the many times she had attempted to enter the house at night without drawing attention to the lateness of the hour only to be thwarted by the cacophony of sounds the old house made. She had made it almost to the banister when a light popped on in the living room, and the voice of her mother broke the already broken silence.

"Wynona, is that you?"

"Yes, Mom. I'm just heading to my room, and I will see you in the morning." She began to walk upstairs, hoping to avoid a long conversation.

"That's good, but I promised Beth that you'd see her for a few moments when you got in." Wynona was still on the stairs, determined to have this conversation as far as possible from her mother.

"But it's late, Mom. Isn't Beth sleeping?" Wynona was desperate to put off seeing Beth until she had prepared herself.

"I promised her I would ask you. Just pop in and say good night. I'm going to bed, and I will see you for breakfast." Mrs. Swanson appeared at the bottom of the staircase, ascended the steps, stopped for a moment to give Wynona a kiss on the cheek, and whispered in her ear, "Good to have you home." She then disappeared into the darkness. This left Wynona without her chief excuse because she would not be required to have any conversation with her mother, so she slowly walked back down the stairs and turned the corner to the study. The door of the study was ajar, and she could see that there was a soft light in the room. She opened it farther to see her sister in a hospital bed. An IV bag hung on a pole next to her. The night stand beside her bed was filled with bottles and pill cases, with a Bible and several books just off to the side. Beth's head was turned away from the door, and Wynona noticed that the light came from a Winnie-the-Pooh nightlight imported from Wynona's bedroom. She thought to herself that she had spent many a night trying to secretly read by the light of that nightlight. Wynona quietly slipped into a chair that was pulled up by the bed, and she gazed at Beth.

Beth was a blond beauty who everyone had always loved, not so much for her beauty but for her beautiful spirit. It would have been easy for Wynona to be jealous of her if it had not been so impossible. It was impossible because Beth was as humble as she was beautiful. Wynona couldn't recall a single time when Beth put her own desires above another or said a thoughtless or unkind word. Not that it didn't happen—Beth was not a saint—but the times it did happen were such an aberration that they simply were not noticed. She had not married although she'd had many chances with many men who wanted her undivided affection. For whatever reason, she had found that loving life, all of life, was way too consuming. It didn't leave time for romance. Her chosen profession was teaching, and she could have taught anywhere at any school, but she chose to come back to Brandstad and teach the second grade. And now here she was, lying before Wynona, silent and dying. The light in the room seemed to cause her to have a sacred, unearthly glow. Wynona felt her heart about to burst as she reached out to gently stroke Beth's hair.

"Boo!" Beth turned her head with a jerk, and Wynona slipped off her chair onto the floor. "Thought I was dead, eh?"

Wynona didn't know whether to kiss her or hit her as she crawled back onto the chair. She was thunderstruck. Finally able to get her heart out of her throat and back into her chest, she muttered, "OK, you got me, but you sure had to work hard to do it!"

"I heard you come in...You still walk like an elephant," she said with a warm smile.

"Better than looking like one." Wynona again reached out to Beth and put her hand on hers. "Hear you've been feeling a bit peevish lately. We've got to put an end to that. Lady Beth must ride again."

When the two were children, they made up stories that took them into distant lands full of fantastic creatures. Beth was Lady Beth of the Woods who could speak to all the woodland creatures, and they would do her bidding. The squirrels would chatter away in the trees, and Beth would listen and carry on a very respectable conversation with them, often chiding them for not being more generous with sharing their nuts. The birds would also seem to appear from every-where when Beth walked through the forest, and Beth would often interpret their stories to her little sister, who would listen with rapt attention. Sometimes Wynona would forget that it was all a game because it seemed that Beth did have some magical ability to be a friend of all that was in the forest. She loved all animals, big and small, but Beth's favorite forest creature was the butterfly. Wynona remembered hours of ecstasy exploring the woods and chasing vari-ous colored butterflies. As Beth walked in the forest meadows, it was common to see butterflies lightly flitting about her head and gently resting upon her as if she was one of them. In fact, Wynona found it difficult sometimes to separate her childhood fantasies from the reality of her actual youth. Did the animals actually speak to Beth? Did the butterflies dance about her like she was a fairy queen? Clearly that is how she remembered it, but the adult Wynona knew that those things could not have happened.

In these fantasies, Wynona was Wynona the Water Princess. Her special abilities included talking to sea creatures and swimming like a mermaid. The two girls would spend hours creating their stories and illustrating them with watercolor drawings. They would even make up songs and sing them as they walked in the nearby woods, imagining themselves living out their stories. As they grew older, these childhood fantasies gave way to the realities of growing up. Still, Wynona and Beth never forgot these magical days and cherished the memories. Beth, as an elementary-school teacher, brought the story of the Lady of the Woods and the Water Princess into her classroom and held the class spellbound during their favorite hour of the day—storytime. Her childlike fantasies awakened the children's imaginations, and they burst forth in their own personal fantasies. This endeared Beth to her students because they knew she was actually one of them, only older and wiser.

Wynona, on the other hand, had long ago packed up those years like a grieving mother would the baby clothes of her deceased child. They were too precious to throw away but too painful to look at and remember what she had lost. The world that Wynona now lived in was full of numbers, deadlines, and scratching her way to the top. There was no room for butterflies in a room full of spiders. She had learned that life was a series of losses that had to be overcome in order to move on. Where she was moving on to, she really didn't know, but what she did know was that if she stopped moving, the pain would catch up with her. That was why she did not return to Brandstad and why, if not for Beth's illness, she would still be avoiding her hometown at all costs. But now that she was here, she knew she must somehow endure it and return unscathed to her real life.

Beth took a long look at Wynona. "You look tired, Sis."

"Been driving all day to see you...but hey, how're you doing?" Wynona never liked it when Beth took one of those knowing looks at her. It always made her feel naked on the inside, like Beth was seeing past the carefully contrived exterior right into her soul.

"Never been better. Gonna run a marathon tomorrow. Join me?" Beth's words were noticeably quieter now, and Wynona could see for the first time that the perpetual strength that was one of her chief attributes was not there.

"I'll pass, but I will see you in the morning."

"You were always more about swimming than running." Beth closed her eyes and began to fade into a soft sleep. Wynona got up to leave, and with her eyes still closed, Beth whispered, "So glad you're here. I've been worried about you, Sis, but it's all going to be OK now that you're home."

Beth then fell into a quiet sleep. Before Wynona left the room, she looked back at Beth one more time. The drapes were open, and the moon cast its silvery light upon Beth's face. Wynona could see that she had a slight, almost sly smile on her face. A queer feeling came over her. She had seen that smile before, but when was it? Beth had thousands of expressions, and growing up, it was completely possible to tell exactly what she was thinking by simply studying them. Then Wynona remembered where she'd seen that look before. It was when they played hide the treasure. This was a game they had made up, where Beth would hide something valuable like a piece of candy or a small gift in their room, and Wynona would come in and try to find it. But Beth wasn't very good at it, because she just couldn't contain her excitement when Wynona got near the treasure. She would always give away the location by that same smile. All Wynona had to do to find the treasure was keep one eye on Beth and walk about the room. When the smile came out, she knew she was near the treasure.

Seeing Beth like this had been a shock, and the thoughts surrounding their meeting swirled in her head as she found her way to her old bedroom. As expected, it had not changed in the slightest since she'd left it eight years ago. Wynona undressed quickly and crawled into her old bed, hoping that she could quickly fall asleep. As tired as she was, she would have, had it not been for the one image that would not leave her. She couldn't put out of her mind's eye the picture of Beth lying in the moonlight. But more specifically, she was puzzled by that old familiar smile. "Why was she smiling? What treasure could she possibly have hidden?" she mumbled. As she fell into a restless sleep, Wynona couldn't help but feel that there was far more to this visit than she was prepared to face.

6
Wynona Meets the LARPs

WYNONA WOKE TO a sound that she was completely unaccustomed to hearing, the sound of...nothing. No sirens, no traffic noise, no sounds from the neighbors through the thin walls of her apartment building. There was only the occasional birdsong, but even the birds seemed to be keeping it at a reasonable decibel level. Some might think that this would be relaxing, even invigorating, but not Wynona. To Wynona it was disturbing. Somehow the noise of the city helped her mute the noise in her head, and now that the city noise was absent, she had nothing to insulate herself from her thoughts. She lay there a few minutes, wondering how she was going to endure the deprivation, when she heard the first sounds of civilization. It was kitchen noises from downstairs, and she caught the quintessential breakfast smell, bacon. Now for most everyone in the universe, the wafting aroma of bacon cooking would be deliriously delicious and could single-handedly propel one out of bed, but for Wynona, it meant only one thing, so she groaned and put her head under the pillow. She knew what always accompanied that smell. Any moment, her mother would come bursting through the door carrying a tray laden with fried animal flesh, oversalted, cheesy eggs, and watery orange juice made from concentrate. Everything that Wynona hated. But the worse part of it would be that her mother would sit on the edge of the bed waiting for her to eat it and expecting praise for putting her through the ordeal. Then would come the thousand and one questions about her work, her friends, her boyfriends, and whether or not she had found a good church to attend. All of which Wynona would answer in monosyllabic words of yes or no. Even now she thought she could hear the dreaded plates being put on the tray, and she thought that this had to be what a condemned man felt like when he heard his last meal approaching. There was only one thing to do: beat her mother to the punch. Maybe, she thought, if she could get to the kitchen before the foul feast was served, she could be spared. So she threw off her covers, put on an old robe she found still hanging in the closet, and ran downstairs to the kitchen just in time to see her mother putting the finishing touches on her surprise.

"Oh, you're up already. I've almost got your breakfast ready." June looked up from grating thin slices of yellow cheese over a frying pan of steaming scrambled eggs and smiled.

June was her name, and June was her personality. Just like the month, June always seemed to be full of sunshine and blossoming flowers; it made Wynona sick. Wynona needed more than smiles and platitudes from June when she was growing up. She was deeply wounded by her father's death and never felt comforted by the banalities spewing from her mother. Wynona likened her mother to the figurines June kept in a glass case in the living room—every one a plump, smiling little Bavarian child in lederhosen or a peasant skirt walking hand in hand or playing with their furry little dogs. Life was never like that for Wynona, and no matter how hard she tried, she couldn't make her mother see that the more cheerful she was, the farther and faster Wynona wanted to run away. But now here she was, trapped in the domain of eternal sunshine and lollipops.

"Mom, I don't eat breakfast. Coffee is enough."

"You don't eat breakfast? But it's the most important—"

"Meal of the day. Yes, I know, but I have never eaten breakfast, and I don't want it now, so please, just some coffee." June gave Wynona the sort of look a golden retriever gives when told it is not going to be taken on a walk.

"How about just one slice of toast?"

Wynona saw that she was not going to escape without consuming something for breakfast, so she relented. "OK, a slice of toast."

"I've got some good lingberry preserves."

Wynona shot her a look that told her what she could do with her lingberry preserves, and June quickly put coffee and two pieces of dry toast in front of her daughter. Wynona broke off a small piece of toast and crunched it loudly. "*Mmm*, good toast!"

June smiled and ignored the obvious sarcasm. "The hospice nurse is in with Beth right now, but she would love to see you when you're through."

"Hospice? Who called hospice? Is everyone giving up?" Wynona was shaken by the finality of the situation she'd stepped into.

"She's been fighting for months. It was her decision," June said with a sigh of resignation.

"We'll see about that." Wynona took a gulp of coffee and headed off to Beth's room just as the hospice nurse was leaving.

"Oh, Wynona, Beth has told me so much about you," said the woman, who appeared to be in her midsixties. She had gentle eyes and a comforting voice.

"Did she tell you that I don't believe in quitting?"

"Well, she said that you'd have a hard time with her illness."

"Really? You think I may have a *hard time* with letting my sister die?" Wynona said sarcastically. She then pushed past the nurse without further conversation and stepped into Beth's room.

"Well, hello, little miss sunshine." Beth was propped up on some pillows with a small plate of cheesy scrambled eggs in front of her.

"If you're going to have a last meal, couldn't you have picked something, anything, better than that?"

"You know Mom. She's especially proud of her cheesy scrambled eggs, so I oblige her," she said with a wink and a smile. "And before you go off on one of your patented diatribes on not accepting the status quo, you've got to know that we tried everything, short of exchanging this body for someone else's, so please, let's not ruin our time together with your stubbornness." She took a small bite of eggs. "That is, unless you are volunteering to donate the use of your body, in which case, I would need to have a complete list of all your risky behaviors for the past six years...including boyfriends. I need to know what I'm getting, you know."

Wynona was dumfounded. She felt like she had walked into a death-row cell where the prisoner was passively waiting for the sentence to be carried out. No, even worse, the prisoner was actually happy she was going to die. Wynona sat down on the chair, deflated from her previous emotion, and mumbled, "I don't do hopeless. You know that."

"Who said hopeless?" Beth motioned for Wynona to crawl up on the bed and sit next to her. "Come here and help me with these." She picked up a forkful of eggs.

Wynona slowly pulled herself up onto Beth's bed and gave a nauseated look at the eggs. "And I definitely don't do those."

It was then that Wynona could see Beth's room in full daylight for the first time. Every inch of her walls was filled with pictures of butterflies made out of colored construction paper; some even hung from the ceiling in mobiles like they were in flight. "Looks like your room has been attacked by a flock of butterflies."

"Oh, that's my kids. They know how much I love them." Beth put her hands on Wynona's and spoke in a more serious tone. "Wynona, you've got to help me."

"Help you? Sounds more like you've given up."

"If you mean that I know I'm going to die, yes, I've accepted that."

"But why? I'm sure we can we can find a new procedure or another doctor. Something, anything, that keeps you from..." Wynona couldn't get herself to say the word *dying*, because it was too final.

"Maybe they could give me a few months, but at what price? I'm not afraid of dying. We're all going to face it someday. I'm just facing it sooner than most." She could see that this was very hard for Wynona to hear, so she pulled her closer and whispered, "I need you to help me do it well."

Wynona bolted upright. "If you mean you want me to pull the plug or something, I'm not—"

Beth put her cool hand on Wynona's flushed cheek. "No, sweetie, I just mean that I want to make sure that when I go, there's nothing unsaid or undone, OK?"

Wynona cast her eyes down. "You're asking me to sit back and watch you die?"

Beth looked into the tortured face of her sister for a moment until Wynona raised her head to meet her sister's eyes. "No, I'm asking you to help me live fully in whatever time I have left." Beth, now noticeably weaker, slipped down into a more comfortable position on the bed. "I think I'm going to take a little nap, and you think about it. I know—why don't you take a walk in the woods. You always loved to walk in the woods. It will do you good." Beth fell asleep, leaving Wynona to remove the breakfast tray and pull the covers up around her neck. Wynona left Beth's room and headed back to the kitchen where she dropped off the tray. June was busy at the sink washing dishes.

"How's Beth?" she asked without turning around.

"How do you think she is? Apparently she's dying, and nobody is doing anything about it."

Still at the dishes, her mother said, "Remember that you're just coming into this. Beth's been at this for quite a while."

"And that's another thing. Why didn't anyone let me know how sick she was? I had a right to know!"

June finally turned around and leaned against the counter. "It was the way Beth wanted it. She knew you'd come charging in and take command and probably ruin your career with that company you work for. So she waited until she knew one way or the other."

"That wasn't her call. I had a right to know!" Wynona said, speaking more out of frustration than anger. "Why didn't you tell me?"

"I really wanted to, if for no other reason than to get you to come and visit once, but she wouldn't let me, and Beth can be just as stubborn as you when she's made up her mind. But you're home, and now there're no secrets." June folded up the dish towel, gave Wynona a kiss on the cheek and headed for the door.

"Where are you going?"

"I've got the shop to tend, so I'll see you for dinner."

"You're just going to go off and leave Beth alone?"

"Honey, we've got it all worked out. It's become a routine. The nurse will be popping in later this morning, and someone from church will come by with lunch and spend time with Beth, and then I'll be home this afternoon. Beth sleeps most of the day anyway because of the meds." By this time, June had put on her jacket and grabbed her purse.

"What about me? What am I supposed to do?"

"You'll figure something out. But don't hang around the house all day. Beth wouldn't like you to do that, and I don't think it would do you much good either. Short visits with Beth work the best." June then was out the door, and Wynona was left standing in the kitchen with the unsettling feeling that she was the only one who had nothing to do. For Wynona, that was a very unusual experience because she had become an expert at filling in even the tiniest crack in her schedule. She abhorred silence and inactivity. Wynona checked on Beth and found she was sleeping, so she decided to do what Beth had suggested and go for a walk in the woods. She thought the fresh air and brisk walk would help clear her head from all that had happened over the past twenty-four hours.

After dressing in sturdy hiking clothes, Wynona drove out to where she and Beth had passed so many wonderful summer days.

About five miles outside of town, the river flowed swiftly through several small, narrow valleys before it came to the flatlands farther west and slowed to a gentle, meandering pace. The two sisters would strap picnic lunches to their bikes and spend countless carefree hours climbing the bluffs overlooking the river and exploring the small caves that pockmarked the area. During one of their adventures, they found an especially exquisite little valley that could only be accessed by a steep trail. Wynona determined that this valley would be the best place to get her head together. If any place in the world was sacred to Wynona, it was that place.

Wynona followed the county road to just past the train trestle that spanned the river. There, she turned onto a dirt road and followed it for about a mile and a half until it ended in a small open space cut out of a stand of trees. From there, it was another half-mile hike up a small unmarked trail around one hill, then to the top of another larger hill where she could look down on the deep, narrow valley. It was as she remembered it—green and lush and bursting with summer grasses and flowers impatient to make their appearance after a long winter's sleep. She stepped away from the path and sat on a lovely protruding rock, where she had a commanding view up and down the small valley. She could see the tributary stream flowing down the center on its way to join the main river several miles away. Though summer had arrived, the air was cool. She turned her face toward the sun to absorb its warmth and gave herself over to the quiet solitude of the moment. She took off her small backpack, lay back on the warm rock, and closed her eyes. The only sounds to be heard were the faint echoes of dancing waters in the valley and the songs of the birds as they called out to one another. But then another sound came to her, an unnatural sound that did not fit in these quiet surroundings: the sound of metal clanging from somewhere behind her. "Damn," she said out loud as she bolted upright and turned to where she thought the noise had originated. It seemed to be coming from down the path that she had hiked in on. Wynona was not in the mood for company and was angry that she might have to share her solitude with someone else, so she got up and found cover in sur-rounding trees where she could clearly see the path yet not be seen.

The first thing she saw was someone who looked like an Indian, but on closer inspection, Wynona decided he looked more like something from an action-comic magazine. His long blond hair was pulled back into a ponytail, and he had on animal-skin clothing and a large sword strapped to his back. Following closely behind him was a woman in what could only be described as a filmy, diaphanous garment, which caused her to look like something between Tinker Bell and one of Robin Hood's Merry Men. She was followed by a tall, hooded monk who walked silently, taking long, loping strides. After the monk, the source of the noise was revealed in the form of a pudgy little fellow dressed like...Wynona actually couldn't tell what he was dressed like because she was not familiar with dwarf attire. As they came closer, she suddenly realized who they were. They were the same group of ex—high school friends she had seen at Bill's restaurant the night before. It was all she could do to keep from letting go with a laugh because the sight was too ridiculous to be believed. The only one she did not recognize was the hooded monk, because his face was obscured. She decided he must be just as much a loser as the rest of them.

The band of costumed characters continued on the trail past the overhanging rock that Wynona had been on and headed down into the valley. The little dwarf was still having a difficult time keeping up. He seemed to be having trouble with his belt slipping and needed to stop and adjust it every few yards.

Wynona's anger dissipated as her curiosity increased. Was this some sort of strange comic-book cult? She couldn't resist shadow-ing them to see what they were up to. Because Wynona had been an outcast in her youth, she had sought solace in the woods and would take long solo hikes to avoid any contact with other humans. She would often wander these woods alone, and even if she encountered others, she would disappear with the skill of an experienced woodsman. Because of her isolation, she usually felt more at home in the forest than she did with people. Her skill in the forest became so good that she could walk silently and unseen if she wanted to. She had wondered if she had lost this talent by living in the city, but now that she was reunited with her old haunts, the skills seemed to have come back to her quickly. The group was almost out of sight as she emerged from her place of concealment and began to shadow their movements on the trail by always staying just above them and out of sight. After several minutes on the trail, the group emerged at the valley, where they stopped and formed a circle.

Wynona was just out of earshot, but she was so consumed with curiosity and confident in her ability to be stealthy that she was determined to find a place where she could hear what they were saying. She saw that the other side of the valley offered a better chance for eavesdropping, so she continued about a hundred yards farther downstream where she knew there was a place to cross. From there she worked her way back upstream to the hiding spot she had chosen. This took her about fifteen minutes. The last hundred feet she crawled the entire way into her concealed observation place. She slowly pulled out her cell phone and worked herself into a position where she could get a picture, reasoning to herself, "They're never going to believe this at the office unless I have pictures."

Connor, apparently quite agitated, was pacing around the group, occasionally stopping in front of one of the members to make his point. "If he's out there, then we've got to find him! Think of the experience points if I kill a dragon!"

"All we know is that there was an empty pen with a name on it." Lori spoke in a lower voice, trying to calm Connor.

"But what about the tracks? My dad said there were tracks that went into the forest. That means there was something there, and it was big." Connor unsheathed his sword and began to slash at the air.

"If it's that big, then maybe we should get a gun or something." Kyle was always nervous whenever Connor began getting aggressive with his sword. These fears may have been caused by many painful encounters when they were in high school and Connor was on the opposite end of the social food chain. Or perhaps he truly felt that Connor was going to do himself or someone else major damage by his utter lack of swordsmanship. Kyle finally couldn't take it anymore and shouted, "Could you put that away. You might hurt someone."

"That's the idea, doofus." Connor took a swing that came within an inch of Kyle's head.

"His name is Brummel, and you should put the sword away unless you plan on using it for some good purpose." The one who was speaking was the man in the hooded robe, and he stepped in front of Kyle.

"Who made you the boss?" Connor took an aggressive stand and began to make wide circles with his sword in front of the hooded man.

Wynona, transfixed by the surreal quality of this conversation, was now realizing that something seemed very dangerous about it. She knew Connor's reputation in high school was that he was a violent semisociopath who only escaped from being jailed numerous times because of his father's interventions. Apparently, that behavior had not changed in the eight years she'd been away. Until this time, Wanderer had remained hooded, but now, she saw him step toward Connor and pull back his hood. Wynona gasped audibly because it was Brandon, her one and only teenage boyfriend. Knowing that she may have just revealed her location, she threw herself down on the ground and hoped that no one had heard her. She really didn't need to worry, because the group was entirely focused on the confrontation between Brandon and Connor.

"We are all equals here, and we will treat each other with respect." Brandon took his staff and waved it across his body so that it transformed from walking stick to fighting staff.

Connor saw this as a challenge and brought his sword up, pointing it at Brandon's face. "Bring it on, monk boy!"

They stood for several moments, staring at each other, until Lori broke the standoff by strolling over to Connor and running her hand down the arm that was holding the sword. She nudged up against him. "OK, boys, let's keep it civil here. We need to decide what to do about this dragon or whatever it is. I like Perales's idea. We capture it or kill it. Who knows. It could hurt someone. We might become heroes." Lori had found that she could exert more power through her feminine wiles, overcoming any masculine muscle. This was a skill she used liberally and often.

The tension had been broken, and Brandon took a few steps toward Wynona's hiding place with his head bowed in thought. He came to the place where she was lying and would have stepped upon her if he had walked any farther, but he suddenly stopped and turned around to address the group.

"I have determined to go on a quest to find the dragon and to bring it no harm." Brandon planted his staff in front of himself with a snap that punctuated his sentence.

"And I will kill it when I find it, and you can't stop me." Connor was emboldened by Lori's taking his side.

Brandon stepped away from the group and made a gesture. "Then I will seek the dragon without you. Who else will go with me?"

Kyle spoke up. "You can't go alone. That would break the fellowship, and we're supposed to do these things together."

Brandon looked at Kyle and spoke in a softer voice. "A quest is sacred and cannot be undertaken for vain glory or selfish motives. I joined this fellowship because I wanted to explore the world of wonders that are hidden from us in our everyday lives. If you turn this quest into a way to win contests or improve your standing, then I must turn away from you."

"Screw you. You're a queer, and you've always been a queer, but if you think you're going to find whatever is out there before I do, then you're even more of a queer than I think you are, and that's really, really queer."

"Well spoken, Perales. You have again shown the depth of your reasoning and wit. It looks like Alliea has chosen. What about you, Brummel?"

Lori went over to Kyle and put her arms around his shoulders. "Oh, he's coming with us, right, Brummel? After all, we're going to end up with all those experience points, you know?" When Lori turned on her charms, few men could resist, but Kyle was especially vulnerable because he had no experience with feminine attention.

Kyle lowered his head and nodded.

"Then I will go alone," Brandon said and began to walk away.

"Oh, you won't be alone, because I'm going to make sure that even if you do find that dragon thing, I'll get it before you can do anything with it. Do you hear me?" Brandon did not respond but walked back up the path and out of sight.

Kyle shuffled his feet and moaned. "Great, what are we going to do now? We've lost our wizard."

"Screw him. We don't need him. We're going to get so many experience points from killing a dragon that we'll buy ourselves another wizard." Connor began to pace again. "But we've got to have a plan."

Lori moved back to Connor. "Why don't you all come over to my house tomorrow night, and we'll discuss our next move."

"Your house? Your father hates us," Connor said as he grabbed Lori by the waist.

"I can handle my father." They began walking up the same path that Brandon had.

Connor looked at his watch. "Crap! I've got to go to work!"

"Hey, you're not supposed to have a watch." Kyle didn't really like confrontation, but in his own passive way, he made sure that Connor knew he was violating the rules of LARPing.

"So tell me, little man, how am I supposed to tell the time? Look at the sun?" Connor's statement was meant to be facetious, but Kyle didn't know the difference.

"Well, yeah, sort of. You see, when the sun is—"

But Connor didn't have the patience for Kyle's failure to identify social cues. "I'm out of here!" Connor started up the trail, and the others followed while Kyle still tried to explain the movement of the sun.

When they had gone, Wynona slowly picked herself off the ground and dusted the dirt from her clothes. She walked over to the area the group of LARPers had occupied and slowly tried to comprehend what she had just witnessed. If someone told her they had seen grown people dressed in costumes, calling themselves weird names, and talking about a quest to kill a dragon, she would have said they were high on drugs. But she was stone-cold sober and what she had just seen was no illusion. One thing was for certain—she had dodged a bullet when she dumped Brandon. Not only was he in a go-nowhere town and doing a go-nowhere job, but he was clearly delusional. She actually felt sorry for him in between the times she broke down in laughter.

The sun was now directly over the little valley, and she sat down by the stream and watched the water dance around the rocks and form small eddies of current. As she watched, a leaf came downstream, got caught in an eddy, and began to spin around and around. She picked up a stick and gave the leaf a push so that it was free to resume its journey down the valley to join the river, which would eventually find its way to the sea. She reflected that her life was like that leaf. She had been trapped and madly spinning and was now finally free to find her way to the larger world. But if that was true, why didn't she feel free? In some ways, her life in the city seemed even more confining than when she lived in Brandstad.

After lingering awhile, she thought it would be safe to return up the path to her car. As she hiked along the path, she ruminated on the discussion she had overheard, but one thing about the whole encounter really puzzled her. She could sort of understand why people would want to dress up and do really stupid things in the woods—after all, they were residents of Brandstad. But what didn't make any sense was the discussion about a dragon. Could they really be searching for a dragon? This was the question she turned over and over in her mind as she returned to her car. She could not get the dragon out of her mind, and the more she thought about it, the more she had a strange sensation that she was being watched. "Hmm"—she laughed to herself—"must be the dragon."

The dust followed Connor's car like a huge, dirty vapor trail. Lisa casually smoked a cigarette while Kyle fumbled in the backseat, desperate to fasten his seat belt; however, just as he was about to click it, Connor hit another pothole, and Kyle bounced his head off the roof.

Lisa casually turned to Connor. "What's the rush?"

"My dad said if I were late one more time, he'd fire my ass."

Blowing a puff of smoke Connor's way, Lisa said, "That's better than killing mine. Slow down!"

Kyle was twisting himself around in another vain attempt to find the other half of the seatbelt when he saw a police car with its red lights on. "Hey, guys, there's someone behind us."

Connor hit the accelerator harder. "Well, they can eat my dust."

"I don't think they're going to like that."

Connor looked in the rearview mirror and exclaimed, "Shit!" He pulled over, and the police car stopped behind them. Out stepped Sheriff Joe. He lit a cigarette and walked slowly over to his son's car, peered in, and saw the trio in their full LARP gear.

"Hello, Dad," Connor said sheepishly.

Sheriff Joe took a long look at the three LARPers in the car. "You folks going someplace special?"

Lisa leaned back in her seat. "We just came back from some hiking in the woods, Sheriff."

"Anywhere close to Old Man Stealy's place?"

"Not too far," Connor said.

The sheriff opened the car door. "Step out of the car, son. I need to talk to you."

"But, Dad, I'll be late to work."

"Why should today be any different? Come over here. I want to ask you a question." Connor reluctantly got out of the car, knowing that his father would not be happy seeing his LARP outfit. The sheriff looked his son up and down in his full LARP glory. "Son, do I need to be seriously concerned?" Connor began to answer his father, but the sheriff decided that now was not a good time to have that conversation. "No, don't say anything...I'd rather not know. What I need to ask you is when you were in the woods, did you see anything strange?"

Connor was relieved that he was somehow not the object of his father's questioning. "Strange?"

Sheriff Joe couldn't help but be befuddled by his son, and he was incapable of hiding it. "I can't believe I'm asking you this...yes, any strange tracks or dead animals?"

"Oh, you mean did we see the dragon?"

"Did I say dragon?" Kyle and Lisa were hanging out of the window hoping to listen in on the conversation. The sheriff turned and gave a look that prompted them to duck back into the car. Turning back to Connor, he said, "I only said unusual. Did you see anything unusual?"

Thinking that he had the inside track on the dragon mystery, Connor repeated, "Like a dragon?"

Frustrated at his inability to gather information from his son, the sheriff said, "Forget it...Get out of here." With that, he waved at him to get in his car and muttered to himself, "Is everyone crazy around here?"

As Connor started the ignition, Lisa asked, "What did your dad want?"

"He was wanting to know if we saw the dragon."

Kyle's ears perked up. "So there really is a dragon?"

Connor put the car in gear and slammed down on the accelerator. "Damn right there's a dragon...and we're going to get it."

Another thick cloud of dust flew out from behind Connor's car. Coughing, Sheriff Joe choked out, "I'm worried about that boy."

7
Brandstad

IT WAS A short drive back to town, and Wynona decided to pop in on her mother's store on the way back home. June owned a flower and gift shop in the heart of town. She had purchased it with the insurance money left to her after her husband died. It could not be described as a thriving business, but it did provide just enough to meet her modest needs, and when Beth returned from college to teach at the local school, she helped with the household expenses. Wynona had worked in the shop sporadically in her teens but was never well suited to the glacial pace of Brandstad life. It did however suit June perfectly, because the only customers she saw were those who did not really need to be there, and therefore they were friendly and talkative, which were the conditions in which June thrived. The only time business was more urgent was when she provided flowers for a wedding or a funeral, and then June saw her business as more of a ministry than a way to make money. Truly, June was well suited for her business, and all the town knew it. So when a big-box store opened about twenty miles away in Rock Falls, the folks in town continued to patronize June's gift shop.

Downtown Brandstad was less than three blocks long and consisted of only the essentials. If the townspeople needed anything major, they drove the twenty miles to Rock Falls. Wynona parked her car in front of her mother's shop and decided to take a stroll down Main Street before she visited June. Nothing had changed. The corner gas station still had the option of full- or self-serve on the pumps, but as everyone knew, it really didn't matter which pump you pulled up to, because Hector would pump your gas for you either way, and he would ask if you needed your oil and your tire pressure checked. Wynona thought the town backward when she lived here, but after living in the pragmatic world of business, she'd developed a more cynical view. *He must sell more oil this way*, she thought to herself as she watched him wipe a dipstick. Across the street from the gas station was the only testament to the twenty-first century—an electronics shop, although it had a sign in the window stating they repaired TVs and radios. *Who does that anymore?* Wynona thought as she passed by and looked in the window.

Inside she could see a couple of younger types with white shirts, black ties, and the obligatory pocket protectors. One of them stepped from behind the register, and she noticed it was the dwarf she'd seen only a few hours before. "Oh, this is just too good," she said to herself as she entered the shop.

"Good afternoon. Can I help you find something?" Kyle stepped from behind one of the racks where rows of connectors, plugs, and fasteners hung in neat little bags. His badge read, "Kyle, assistant manager." Wynona couldn't help but notice that he really fit well in this environment, and it was somehow not dissimilar to his woodland character.

"Well, Kyle, I guess I need a charger for my phone." Wynona was not making this up. She had left home without her charger, and all she had was the one that plugged into her car's outlet.

"Our chargers are over here." Kyle walked her over to the cell phone center. "Do you have your phone with you so I can find what type of plug you need?"

"Yes, it's right here." Wynona reached into her jacket pocket and pulled out her phone. As she was holding it out, she had a very diabolical idea. "I'm also having a little problem with the camera on this phone."

Kyle took the phone and looked it over. "I'm really not a smartphone expert. Heck, they come out with a new one every month, but I'll do my best. Can you show me what's wrong with it?"

"Yes, I don't seem to get as sharp of an image as I would like." Wynona took back her phone and brought up the picture of the LARPers she had taken just a few hours earlier. "What do you think?" She handed the phone back to Kyle.

He looked it over, oblivious to the content. "It looks OK to me."

"What about the guy with the sword? Do you think that's really clear?" Wynona was obviously enjoying the game, while Kyle remained clueless.

Wynona took back the phone and then expanded the picture so that Kyle was clearly visible in all his dwarf glory. "What do you think of this one?"

When Kyle saw it, he stumbled back into an assortment of electronics. "Miss, I think your camera works just fine."

Wynona snapped the phone back and looked at it with a smile. "I guess you're right. It must be the subject matter." She reached around Kyle, took a charger off the rack, and headed for the register.

Kyle was so flustered that he stood momentarily dazed against the display until Wynona looked over at him and cleared her throat. He then pulled himself together, scanned the charger, and began to go through his standard sales process.

He avoided looking directly at Wynona. "Do you have one of our frequent customer cards?"

"Do I look like I frequent this place?"

Kyle fumbled with his words and was obviously thrown off his usual routine.

"Sorry. I'm supposed to ask all our customers that question. Will it be cash or credit?"

"Here you go." Wynona handed Kyle her credit card. He finished the transaction and put her charger in a bag and handed it to her. As Wynona turned to leave, Kyle took a deep breath, feeling like he was about to escape this troublesome encounter. But when Wynona reached the door, she turned toward him and in an uncomfortably loud voice asked, "So where does one find a dragon around here?" With that, she threw open the door and resumed her stroll around downtown Brandstad. *Well, that was fun*, she thought as she strolled by Bill's. The smells of cooking drifted out onto the sidewalk, and it was only then that Wynona realized she had not eaten anything all day. She looked in the window and saw Clara working behind the lunch counter. She put her hand against the glass and strained her eyes to see if she could make out who was cooking. Clara clipped an order to the circular rack that stood between the restaurant and kitchen, and then Wynona saw Brandon step over and take the order slip. She thought, *Do I dare go in there?* But after having so much fun with Kyle, she was ready for more—and she was hungry. She walked into the restaurant and sat at the counter in full view of the kitchen while feeling a power that comes with prideful arrogance. Clara swooped over and greeted her warmly.

"Glad to see you're back, sweetie." Clara was a nonstop worker and spoke while she wiped down the counter and put dishes away. She whirled around and stopped in front of Wynona. "So what are you hungry for?"

Wynona didn't bother to look at the menu. "Just give me the chopped salad."

Clara was spinning around to put the order on the rack when Wynona stopped her. "Clara, would you mind if I put a little note on the order for the cook?"

"Oh, I get you," Clara said with a little wink. Clara gave the slip back to Wynona, and she wrote a few words and handed it back to Clara.

"I feel like I'm on one of those love-connection shows." Clara put the order on the wheel and hit the bell. "Order up—way up!" A hand reached over to take the ticket, and Wynona waited to see if there would be any reaction, but nothing happened. Clara whizzed by frequently to see if there was any response to what she assumed was a love note, but there was nothing. Finally the door to the kitchen opened, and out came Brandon holding a chopped salad. He walked over to Wynona and placed the salad in front of her.

"Here's your salad. I assume you're still a vegetarian." Brandon was tall and handsome and had an easy, peaceful way about him. Wynona had always believed there was more to him than he would allow himself to discover, but she was too impatient to wait around until he did.

"Of course. Why do you ask?" Wynona gave Brandon a smug little smile.

"Because I was confused. Do you want your dragon in your salad or on the side?" Brandon's manner and inflection were completely unaffected. Anyone listening would have thought he was asking a completely sensible question.

"But you've got to find one first, don't you? I know. Why don't you go on a…what do you call it…a quest. And when you find it, I am sure that any way you prepare it will be just right. After all, that is what you do, right? You're a cook in a diner." And once again Wynona dug into Brandon to make sure that he remembered her prediction.

But Brandon would not take the bait. He simply looked at her and smiled. "Yes, I prepare food that people eat. I find that a very trusted occupation. People actually trust me enough to prepare the food that they put into their bodies." He pushed the plate of salad a little closer to Wynona. "Bon appétit." Brandon walked back to the kitchen, and Wynona gave her salad a troubled look as she picked through it with her fork. *He wouldn't, would he?*

Deciding not to chance it, she pushed her salad away, took a drink of water, and put enough money down on the counter to cover her salad and a tip for Clara. She walked slowly past the kitchen window and caught sight of Brandon working at the stove. He looked up and gave her a friendly smile then went back to his work. Whatever unnerving effect she had on the little dwarf, Kyle, it was completely ineffective on Brandon.

She thought, *How can he be so smug when he's obviously living in some sort of twisted fantasy world?* Wynona continued her short walk through downtown Brandstad and ended up where she had started—in front of June's Flowers and Gifts. She walked through the front door and was greeted by the happy tinkle of a little silver bell. Wynona hated that bell.

"Oh, you're back. I saw your car and wondered where you'd gotten off to." June was busy arranging flowers in the display case. "Did you meet any old friends?"

"I don't have any old friends, remember?" Wynona began wandering around the store to sneer at the assortment of cute and cuddly stuff that was the heart and soul of June's Flowers and Gifts.

"Nonsense. You've got lots of friends, and they're always asking about you."

Wynona was feeling just hungry enough to be even more ornery than usual. "Name one person who's been asking about me. Don't you remember? The town threw a party when I left."

"That nice young man who works at Bill's comes in often to buy flowers, and he always asks about you."

Wynona, juggling a little ceramic angel, just about let it crash to the floor. "Brandon comes in here? What do you tell him about me?"

"Aren't we touchy? What do you think I tell him? I don't know anything about your life except you live in a big city, have an important job, and never come home. Anyway, you should be happy that someone remembers you and asks about you."

"My life is nobody's business, and I would like it kept that way." Wynona put the angel back on the shelf and began to walk out of the store.

"Honey, let's not fight, not now, not with Beth the way she is." June closed the flower case and stepped toward her daughter.

Wynona put her hand on the doorknob. "I just don't want to be talked about."

"I got it. From now on, if someone asks me about my youngest daughter, I'll say, 'Sorry. I just can't talk about her. It's top secret.' And they'll think you're in the CIA or something like that. Won't that be wonderful?"

"Mom!" Wynona found it impossible to reason with her mother because it always turned into some sort of absurdity.

June walked over to her daughter and tenderly put her hand on her cheek. "OK, honey, I'm sorry. Let's be friends. We're going to need each other, and Beth does not need to see us fighting." The reality of the situation came upon Wynona suddenly and unexpectedly, and she could feel the tears well up in her eyes.

"Mom, I've got to go. I'll see you when you get home." Wynona burst through the door and ran to her car with that damned little bell ringing behind her. In the solitude of her car, she composed herself. "Keep it together, girl. Don't lose it now." She took several deep and slow breaths and practiced the relaxation exercises that she had learned in her yoga class. After a few minutes, she had composed herself enough to drive home, and she parked her car in the driveway. She knew she was not on the verge of breaking into tears, but she was far from being OK. Inside the house her sister was dying, and all she could do was sit and watch. Helplessness was not something Wynona dealt with well. And in all of her short life, this was the most helpless she had ever felt. After a few moments, she decided the only thing she could do was go forward, so she took one more deep breath and stepped out of her car.

8
Wynona Gets Rebuked

WYNONA ENTERED THE house and was greeted by the faint sound of music coming from Beth's room. She didn't recognize the song, but she knew Beth had an eclectic taste in music and would constantly surprise her with the songs she liked. From Bach to the Beatles, Beth seemed to take it all in and find something she enjoyed about it. As she drew closer to Beth's room, Wynona began to make out the voice that was singing; it was the raw, emotionally vulnerable sound of an authentic Negro spiritual with only tinny piano accompaniment. These were the words that struck Wynona's ears as she stepped into the room: "His eyes are on the sparrow, and I know he watches me." Wynona saw Beth with her eyes closed, mouthing the words; her face shone with a deep contentment that belied her circumstances.

Beth opened her eyes, put her finger to her lips, and pointed to the chair next to her bed. Wynona obediently sat down and listened to the rest of the song.

> Why should I feel discouraged?
> And why should the shadows come?
> And why should my heart feel so lonely
> And long for heaven and home

When Jesus is my portion,
My constant friend is He.
His eyes are on the sparrow,
And I know he watches me.
I sing because I'm happy.
I sing because I'm free.
His eye is on the sparrow,
And I know he watches me.

Wynona didn't recognize the raspy voice on the recording, but she felt the power of it, for it was sung by someone who not only believed the words but had also experienced them to the depths of her soul. Wynona had always been uncomfortable with Beth's overtly emotional religion and did not like to be around her when she got into one of her spiritual moods. But she loved her sister and was willing to overlook her naïve philosophy of life, as long as she was not expected to believe it too. Wynona didn't believe in God, Jesus, or miracles any more than she believed in Santa Claus or the Easter Bunny. They were all made-up crutches, meant to deal with the painful reality that life is a series of difficult decisions and experiences to which you can bring whatever meaning you want. She believed that humans were, in essence, purely material creatures who existed within a purely material universe that had been created by no God and therefore had no ultimate moral purpose except what was brought to it by humanity. In other words, we are all making this up as we go along, so we should get the best out of this life because there will be no second chances and no surprises when we die. She and Beth had discussed this for years with neither of them convincing the other of the rightness of her position. Wynona eventually came to understand that some people needed to believe in God in order for their lives to work, so she taught herself to be more tolerant of their weaknesses. This philosophy worked well for Wynona. She even developed a sort of pity for those poor individuals who were so weak as to need some sort of higher power to justify their existence.

Listening to this song in the presence of Beth's impending death was in no way comforting to Wynona. The nearness of death was a cold slap in the face of her religious contempt.

The song was over, and Beth switched off the system with the remote control that was resting on her lap. "My nurse made a mix of some songs she thought I would like. I especially like this one. It's by Ethel Waters. Pretty cool, right?"

Wynona had no desire to get into a debate over religion or Beth's taste in music, so she just shrugged her shoulders.

"So what have you been up to, Sis? Did you get out and take a walk?"

Wynona, hoping to lighten things up, said, "Did I ever. You won't believe what I saw!"

Beth propped herself up as best she could and leaned toward her sister. "Tell me."

"Well, you remember Brandon, my old boyfriend? I saw him and a bunch of other high school losers in the forest pretending they were some kind of comic book characters. I mean, they were dressed up In stuff right out of *The Lord of the Rings*, and they gave themselves ridiculous names and everything." Wynona then went on to describe how she overheard their argument over the dragon and how she made little Kyle wet his pants when she showed him his picture. She then relayed how she'd burned Brandon at Bill's.

Beth listened patiently and watched as Wynona contorted in laughter over her morning's escapades. Finally, when Wynona had laughed herself out, Beth let some silence stand between Wynona's story and her response. Wynona became increasingly uncomfortable with the silence and turned to Beth. "Well, wasn't that crazy?"

Beth sat back slightly and closed her eyes. "So you don't believe in dragons?"

Wynona couldn't believe her ears. What kind of response was that?

"Of course I don't believe in dragons. Nobody believes in dragons." Wynona could not hide her frustration at her sister's incredible response.

Beth still had her eyes closed and spoke in a quiet, confident voice. "I do."

"You what?" Wynona said, still not believing what she was hearing.

"I believe in dragons. I believe there are things like dragons that are beyond our limited understanding, and we need to keep our minds open to them if we are to live life fully. You see, Sis, it's when we close our minds, shut our eyes, and harden our hearts to mysteries like dragons that we cease to live. We merely exist."

Wynona's mind was spinning. She didn't want to get into an argument with her invalid sister, not when she was so physically weak, but she also couldn't agree to this mumbo jumbo about believing in things that weren't real. Finally, she thought of a compromise. "Sis, you're talking philosophy. These idiots were talking about a real dragon...They're looking to capture an actual dragon."

"Exactly. And you should go with them. At least you should go with Brandon and look for it, because I think he's got the best chance of finding it."

Wynona took a deep breath. She did not want to say anything that she was sure to regret. "I am not going to go on some asinine search for something that every sane person knows doesn't exist."

"Fine. Then don't go. The least you should do is go and apologize to Brandon for treating him like that. After all, he's the only one in this town that stood by you, and now you're acting like a jerk." Beth was becoming tired again, and her voice was beginning to trail off at the end of her sentences.

"If you think I'm going to go and humiliate myself in front of him..."

Beth reached over and put her hand on Wynona's. "Honey, this is important. I can't tell you why, but I want you to go back to Bill's and tell Brandon you're sorry."

"But..." Wynona protested.

Beth squeezed her hand with all the strength she could. "Promise me."

Wynona was trapped. She knew that Beth was as stubborn as she herself was when she made up her mind on something, so Wynona dared not refuse her this request, especially in her weakened condition.

"All right, all right. I will."

Beth squeezed her hand tighter. "Apologize?"

"Yes, apologize."

Beth opened her eyes, and Wynona could see a slight smile form on her lips. "Today?"

Wynona smiled back at her big sister. "You know, sometimes you really get on my nerves."

"You know it. Now get out of here, and let me get some sleep." Beth was now whispering as she closed her eyes and slipped off to sleep. Wynona lifted Beth's hand and placed it gently on her bed. She then went out into the living room and collapsed on the couch. *How embarrassing. What did I get myself into?* It was so completely out of character for her to ask for forgiveness from anyone, much less an old boyfriend who was actively looking for a dragon. Wynona lay quietly for several minutes with only the sound of the grandfather clock pendulum to accompany her thoughts. *A dragon? How could Beth believe in dragons? But she seemed to know something that she wasn't telling me. Does she know something about this dragon that Brandon was looking for?* Wynona picked herself up off the couch, grabbed her car keys, and headed for the door. "Better get myself going, or I will never do this. Besides, if Beth wakes up and I haven't done it, there will be hell to pay," she said.

9

The Other LARPers

THE OTHER LARPERS were a strange assortment on the fringe of Brandstad society. The one thing they all had in common was that they were eccentrically spinning through life with no real hope of coming into balance with their community. Connor Reilly had been the center of attention in every setting he entered. He drank in adulation like a drunk takes to his bottle; it was satisfying for the moment, but then he would need more in ever-increasing quantities to achieve the same effect. He was a star quarterback in high school, and he was convinced he would be the next big college star until he went off to state. Unfortunately for Connor, his athletic ability was not matched by his intelligence. In fact, the two aptitudes were polar opposites. The only thing he wanted from college was glory, but when it became abundantly clear to the coaching staff that he was untrainable, Connor was quietly returned to Brandstad with the excuse of a career-ending injury. He then set his sights toward getting on with the sheriff's office. His father was open to the possibility, but when Connor literally shot his toe off during target practice at the police academy, even Sheriff Joe had to agree that putting a weapon in Connor's hands would be a disaster. The next best option for Connor was to be a community-service officer. He liked riding around in a squad car while wearing a nifty uniform and telling people what to do. To Connor, it was just like being a police officer but without paperwork or the responsibility of court dates and the like. The position's primary responsibilities were to serve as a crossing guard for the elementary school and to issue tickets to cars that were parked over the maximum two hours on Main Street. The first duty he enjoyed because he got to flirt with all the young mothers who walked their children to and from school and because schoolchildren were just about the only people he could still impress. The second job he enjoyed because he liked to give out tickets and would often wait by the meters as the time expired just so he could slap a parking citation on windshields. He'd then hang around to see the expressions on the motorists' faces. If some poor citizen had an objection to his heavy-handed manner, it was all the better because that was where his need to dominate really got satisfied. Connor's confrontation with Harry, the jolly, rotund barber, was typical of Connor's interaction with all who questioned his authority. Connor knew that Harry's meter would expire at exactly 2:35, and he also knew that Harry was prone to conversation, which was an occupational hazard, so he positioned himself a few feet away from Harry's car but just out of Harry's sightline. Harry was into one of his stories, and Connor knew from experience that it was at least a five-minute one, and there were only two minutes left on the meter. He began to prefill the ticket so that when the time ran out he would be ready to move. The red flag shot up, and instantly, Connor stepped up to Harry's car and slid the ticket neatly between the windshield and the wiper.

Harry caught the movement out of the corner of his eye. "Hey, Connor, what are you doing? I'm right here!"

Adjusting his sunglasses and putting his ticket pad back in its holster, Connor said, "Yeah, and your car is right here, illegally parked."

"But it just expired. Can't you wait one minute?"

"Oh, one minute?" He then went over to the meter and gave it a slap with his hand. "Did you hear that, Mr. Meter? Harry wants another minute. What is that you say? Oh, I can't say that to Harry. Oh, OK. Harry, the meter says, 'Stuff it, fat man.'"

"I don't care who your father is. You can't treat people like—"

"Sorry, Harry. I'd love to talk, but I've got other things to do." Connor swaggered off down the street toward the elementary school to take on his other responsibility...flirting with the children's mothers.

Lori Summerville was another child of privilege in both money and power. Her father and mother had an arranged marriage. Her father, Fred, made the money, and her mother, Susan, arranged to spend it. Lori was an only child because her mother swore that she would never go through the pain of childbirth again, and she, like Lori, always got what she wanted. Lori had everything she wanted and therefore got nothing she needed. As for Connor, her high school years were her glory days. She was the captain of the varsity cheerleaders and an all-conference gymnast. Her father even paid to have a Hungarian gymnastics coach brought to Brandstad just so Lori could work under an Olympic-caliber professional. That tactic did not end well for Lori, or the school, as the coach turned out to be a lecherous old man who was more interested in eyeing little girls in tights than preparing them for competition. It did, however, confirm in Lori's mind that her physical attributes were the means of manipulating men into getting what she wanted. A scandal ensued when the coach was caught making videotapes of the girls in their locker room. But Fred's money limited the damage, and the coach was quietly put on a plane back to Hungary, with few external consequences. Lori's first stint at the psychiatric hospital started during this time, and since graduation, she had split her time evenly between private colleges and rehab facilities. Her most recent return to Brandstad was after an almost-successful suicide attempt. Since returning, she had been able to string together a few months of sobriety. Lori had no idea what was next for her; living was a day-to-day proposition. Her attraction to Connor was a natural phenomenon, like two black holes collapsing on themselves. If Lori had not been so emotionally fragile and incapable of self-regulation, she would have maneuvered herself into a well-appointed lifestyle in an upscale city apartment. However, she found herself isolated and completely bored in a life that she described as "beyond hideous." She joined the LARP fellowship because it offered an escape from the dull, ordinary, commonplace life that was Brandstad, and she felt there was something exciting about dressing up like an elf and practicing her former gymnastic skills. On a deeper level, Lori secretly wished she was the elf princess she had created. As a little girl, she would shut herself in her bedroom when her parents were screaming at each other and gaze out the window, wishing she could fly away over the tops of the trees and beyond the mountains to another world.

Kyle Horner was the fourth son of the Horner family, which had lived in Brandstad for three generations. His father worked at the lumber mill, as did his father before him, and his mother was a secretary in the county administration office. Kyle grew up with three older brothers who were athletic and popular, so when he came along, their reputations preceded him everywhere he went. He was small and nonathletic, unlike his brothers, so he was considered the weak "sister" of the bunch. Playtime for the brothers always ended with him getting kicked, punched, or humiliated, so he became increasingly isolated from his brothers, preferring to be by himself rather than endure their physical abuse. It was during one of these alone times, when he was fourteen years old, that he came across an old ham radio kit from the 1950s while rummaging through the basement. He asked his father about it, but all his father knew was that it must have been his grandfather's and been moved to the basement out of his parents' garage after his father had died several years earlier.

"Your grandfather always liked that stuff," Kyle's father explained. "But I don't have much use for it. You can have it if you want it." This was all he needed to hear because he was captivated by the kit from first sight. Kyle spent long hours diligently following the instructions and carefully soldering the capacitors and transistors onto the circuit board. He read everything he could get his hands on about ham radios and their operation and was able to construct a workable antenna and scavenge a vintage microphone from the trash bin behind the local radio station. He set up a workbench in one corner of the basement and hurried home after school to work at it long into the evening. Kyle's activities drew little attention from any of the other family members. His parents were happy he'd found something that kept him from getting beaten up by his brothers, and his brothers had absolutely no interest in what confirmed for them that he was a weirdo. Finally, after several months of painstaking labor, the radio was ready to fire up.

It was late in the evening when he carefully unwrapped the vacuum tubes that had been stored in their neat little sleeves for over half a century and plugged them in one by one. He then slowly closed the chassis of the radio, connected the power supply, and pushed the power button. He half expected an explosion, but slowly, the vacuum tubes came to life with a soft, warm glow. Then the speaker began to hiss. He carefully turned the tuner wheel and began to hear faint voices that became clearer as he made minute adjustments to the tuner. For the first time in his short life, he felt like he had accomplished something. What he heard coming from the speaker were voices from places as far apart as Ontario, Canada, and Baton Rouge, Louisiana. And not only did he hear them speaking, but when he pressed the switch on his microphone, some of them also heard him. A world beyond Brandstad opened up to Kyle. He purchased a world map from the local drugstore, placed it above his radio, and marked the places he heard over the radio. Kyle didn't know it, but Brandstad's location made it ideally suited for receiving signals from around the world by catching the atmospheric skip. This experience could have been the launching pad for Kyle into a life of electronic discovery, but that did not happen. The mind will not go where the heart does not allow. Kyle could only see himself through the eyes of his family, who never really saw him as more than a strange, socially awkward boy. He enjoyed his radio and taught himself enough basic knowledge to work at the local electronics store, but could never envision himself doing more. After high school, he moved out of his parents' home into a spare bedroom of an elderly lady for whom he did small jobs around the house for a reduction in his rent. But buried deep inside Kyle was still that fourteen-year-old boy who discovered a magic world one night when he plugged in his grandfather's radio.

The LARPs had all been touched by Beth in some way. This was not unusual, because Beth touched a great number of people in Brandstad. It would be difficult to find anyone in town who hadn't been personally affected by Beth or knew someone who was. For Kyle, Beth was the one who came into his store and always treated him as if he was her special friend. Everyone else seemed to look right past Kyle, but Beth always took time to speak to him—even though they had never been in the same social circles. Another quality of Beth that was unique to her was the way she made others feel about themselves. It may be a little thing, but when other customers came into the store, they always needed to look at his badge to remember his name, but with Beth it was different. She always remembered his name and would seek him out in the store even if she did not particularly need his help. Kyle wished it was because she was sweet on him, but he knew it was just because Beth was sweet, and she treated everyone with that same sweetness.

Lori had had a much deeper and more profound experience with Beth's goodness. It was in her last year in high school when she was going through a particularly difficult time, which wound up in her first stay in the psychiatric hospital. Her parents were not very happy that she couldn't get her act together, and she was too ashamed to reach out to any of her friends. Besides, she knew the quality of her friends, and they were not the kind you turned to when you were vulnerable. It was a lonely black pit for her, and she didn't know if she would ever escape from it. Then she received a visit from Beth. Beth was a few years older and was attending the state college to get her teaching degree. Lori and Beth would have been on the opposite ends of the friendship spectrum if they had even been in the same social environment. Lori couldn't even guess how Beth found out she was hospitalized, much less fathom why she would drive a hundred miles to visit. But Beth seemed to have a knack for saying things and being in places that no one expected. And to these places she would bring warmth, hope, and comfort when it was most needed. The strange thing was that Beth didn't just visit Lori once, but she went back regularly to sit and talk with Lori and bring normality to a very abnormal time of her life. Lori and Beth never became friends in the truest sense of the word. That was primarily because every time Lori was released from the facility, she would return to her old ways and her old friends. Beth was not one to encourage self-destructive behavior, and she would step away from Lori's crazy world when it was clear that Lori needed to learn another life lesson about the consequences of foolish choices. When they would see each other on the street or at a social event, Lori awkwardly avoided Beth because she felt she had somehow squandered the time Beth spent with her. She was also uncomfortable around her because she knew she had no secrets from Beth. Beth had seen her at her lowest and had not recoiled or condemned her, and therefore Lori felt somehow emotionally bare in her presence. Still, Lori knew that Beth would not hesitate to reach out to her in compassion when she was completely unworthy of it.

Beth's connection to Connor was less complicated and also less easily understood. Beth was angry whenever she witnessed any of Connor's vindictive, mean-spirited actions. But people like Beth were not kind because others were good. They were kind because they had chosen a life of kindness in spite of the way others acted. So on a bitterly cold winter day, when Connor was doing his crossing-guard duty with his mind more set on survival than on flirting, Beth reached out to him in a lovely act of kindness. The first time it happened, Connor didn't know what to make of it. He was standing on the corner while it was snowing, shivering in the cold with the wind whistling past his ears and his eyes so blurred that he could hardly see the school, much less any children. He felt a tap on his shoulder and turned to see a smiling Beth with a thermos of hot chocolate and an insulated cup. "The kids and I thought you might need something hot to drink, so we made this for you." She then put the cup in his hands and poured hot chocolate into it. "Thank you for all you do to keep my kids safe." With that, she tucked the thermos under his arm and trudged through the snow and back to her classroom. In Connor's twisted mind, she did this because she was attracted to him, and this was her way of getting his attention. But as the days went by, he noticed that she never acted even remotely like she wanted more from him than a respectful friendship. This was very confusing to Connor because all his encounters with the opposite sex were based upon getting what he wanted from them. He naturally assumed that if she did something for him, she wanted something. This was not Beth's way. She always gave without expecting anything in return.

Though it may seem like Beth was a perfect saint, she was not. She struggled to be kind and forgiving, like most people. But Beth had a connection with God's heart that was rare, beautiful, and argumentative. Her conversations with God were often contentious, with her saying no to his promptings and God pressing upon her until she finally relented. Beth did not want to take the hot chocolate to Connor on a cold winter morning. It took everything she had not to get physically ill every time she saw him. She had comforted far too many crying girls who had been used up and thrown away by men like Connor to have any natural affection for him. If it were up to her, he would stand out in the cold until the most precious part of his anatomy froze off. But it was not up to her, and she had fought the hard battle to look past the selfishness of men's actions to see the brokenness of their hearts. So when she was prompted to show kindness to Connor, she reluctantly obeyed.

Another example of this sensitivity was when she received God's request that she visit Lori in the hospital for the first time. Her answer was not an immediate yes. She had a thousand good reasons for not driving a hundred miles to visit someone she hardly knew. She had argued with God right up to the very moment she parked in front of the hospital and all the way to the front desk. There she had to explain that she was not family and not a close friend; she really didn't have any relationship with the patient. It was a miracle that she was allowed to visit Lori the first time. Beth was also absolutely certain that when she did finally sit down with Lori, there would be nothing to say, and Lori would tell her to go home. Indeed, the first visit was awkward, with Lori saying things like, "Tell me again why you drove all this way to spend time with someone you hardly know?" But eventually, after the third or fourth visit, Lori came to believe that Beth really had no other motives than that she genuinely cared and that she truly just wanted to help her through that very rough time in her life.

Beth's kindness to Kyle was more subtle and therefore more indicative of how Beth was to everyone she knew. If you were to ask her why she was so attentive to a person that others simply ignored, she would probably not have understood the question, since she would argue she was not particularly attentive to that person, any more than anybody else. But to understand Beth is to examine the first time she met Kyle in the electronics shop. It was a hot summer day, and she was running a few errands for her mother. One of these tasks was to pick up an extension cord for the living room. She knew what she wanted and would have been able to duck in, purchase it, and move on to the other items on her list quite easily. In fact, she had found just what she wanted when she heard an argument coming from the cash register. Nels Peterson was reaming out the young man at the register for a mistake he had made. Apparently, he had recommended a plug that was the wrong size, which meant Nels had to make a second trip to the store to correct this egregious error. Nels was not known as a patient man, and he was easily angered by anything that even remotely appeared to be incompetence. Beth knew this because she had Nels's son, Tommy Peterson, in her class, and she had seen the boy's little spirit being beaten down by the perfectionistic standards of his father. She had attempted to speak to this issue at the parent-teacher conference but found her suggestions rebuffed. Turning to Mrs. Peterson, she saw the same wounded spirit and determined it was futile to attempt a change in the home. She put her focus on Tommy and made sure that her classroom was a place of exploration, freedom, and encouragement, where he would know what it was like to be believed in. As a result, Tommy's work was much improved, for which Nels took full credit.

Beth overheard the argument at the register, which finished with Nels slamming the plug down on the counter and storming out of the shop, vowing never to come back. Kyle was left staring down at the plug, when from the back room emerged John, the owner of the store, to deliver another beating. This was painful for Beth to listen to, and her heart broke for the young man behind the counter. John eventually retreated to the back room after making very certain that Kyle knew that his job was on thin ice and that if he didn't give better customer service, he would be replaced by a more capable employee. This was the turning point for Beth. She knew exactly what she should do but began debating with herself. She had a long list and a busy day. She could have just said, "It's not my problem," and quickly moved on to her next errand, but that was not the way Beth operated. She took a deep breath, placed the extension cord back on the shelf, and stepped up to a very dejected Kyle and asked to be shown to the extension cords. Kyle hardly looked up and shuffled off to the corner of the store where there was an assortment of wires and cords. Beth knew exactly what she wanted but instead began to ask

Kyle questions. Beth was a master of the question. That was probably why she was such an excellent teacher. She knew that she could
open a mind and lift a spirit better with a well-crafted question than
with anything else. She asked what the difference was in gauges, why
there were some with three prongs and some with two, and if there
was any significance to the colors, along with a dozen other inquiries
all designed to bring out Kyle's competence. With each question, Kyle
seemed to grow in confidence, and his crushed spirit came back to
life. After about fifteen minutes of learning everything one would
ever need to know about extension cords, Beth made her selection
and paid for it at the counter where just a few minutes before Kyle
had been crucified and left for dead. But Beth's kindness did not end
there. She asked Kyle to go and get the owner because she needed to
talk to him. This wasn't what Kyle wanted to hear. He didn't think he
had done anything wrong, but at that point, he felt like he never did
anything right. So he timidly went to fetch his boss, hoping this was
not going to be the last straw. John emerged with Kyle once again
from the back room and prepared himself to hear another complaint
about his incompetent employee. Instead, Beth looked him straight
in the eyes and said, "Sir, I just need to let you know exactly what
I think of your employee. I have rarely received such attentive and
professional service in my life. You have a truly remarkable employee
in"—and here Beth looked at Kyle's badge for the first and the last
time—"Kyle, and I will make sure I do all my shopping here in the
future." Beth then took her extension cord and walked out of the
shop, leaving Kyle in a radiant glow and his boss in hazy disbelief.

Beth had learned, through much trial and error, that if she would pay
attention to that still, small voice in her heart, it would never let her
down. Following that voice was not always easy, and sometimes it
seemed to backfire. Many times, she got strange stares from people,
or was misunderstood by someone she was sent to help. But when
she obeyed the voice, she would always feel an indescribable sense of

peace and completeness. It had been that way when she felt strongly that she should not call Wynona when first learning of her illness, and it had been that way when she finally asked June to call her sister to come home. Beth would say, "God's timing is always perfect," and she believed that whatever was going to happen in Wynona's life, it would be in God's hands and it would happen when and where he wanted.

10
Brandon, Beth, and Wynona

THE RELATIONSHIP BETWEEN Brandon and Beth was completely different than that between any of the other LARPers. Beth was more like a big sister to Brandon ever since he dated Wynona. It was Beth who suggested that he volunteer at the animal shelter and consider becoming a veterinarian. Beth was a seed planter; that was why she made such a good teacher. She saw the potential in each of her students and would always find something to praise and extol. When Wynona left Brandstad, it was not easy for Brandon. Her berating words cut him deeply, and he struggled to find his place in the world. Brandon had been a sensitive boy who felt more deeply than most and therefore was more susceptible to pain. He was probably attracted to Wynona because he also grew up without a father; his parents divorced when he was an infant, and his father had decided that the end of the marriage was also the end of his obligations as a father. Since Wynona was an outcast, it made him think she was a kindred soul. But he discovered that she was not interested in souls, kindred or any other kind, and wanted only to escape what she considered the prison of Brandstad. Still, something connected them, and they both knew it. If Wynona had been a little more empathic or Brandon a little more assertive, they might have been able to maintain a relationship, but Brandon constantly disappointed Wynona, and Wynona consistently wounded him.

Beth saw past Wynona's hardness and always felt that Brandon would be a good match for her if he could somehow find himself and his passions. So every chance Beth got, she would go into Bill's and talk to him about his interests and dreams in the hopes that he would make some slight progress toward them. Beth connected him with the local animal shelter because she knew he had a love for animals and that somehow the neglected shelter animals could be the means of healing the wounds in his spirit. Brandon came alive at the shelter. It was as if he had found a family he never knew, and he was able to be a vital help to those who had been abandoned. Beth and Brandon also occasionally talked about Wynona, and Beth was able to help Brandon see that her spiteful words came from a place that was still grieving her father. This was hard for Brandon to understand, but he was beginning to soften when Beth suddenly became sick, and Wynona returned and opened old wounds.

When Brandon told Beth about joining the LARP community, she was a bit skeptical. It sounded more like escapism than moving forward in life. But as Brandon described the joy he felt in walking the woods and exploring a world beyond this one, Beth became warm to the idea. She could not endorse the other LARPers' motives, but she knew that Brandon was reaching out with tentative hands toward something he could neither fully comprehend nor describe. She knew that whenever this happened, only good things came if one kept his or her heart committed to love and truth. Brandon would describe his encounters in the woods with the other LARPers with such rapturous joy that it began to fascinate Beth. She was even tempted to create a character and join him but reasoned that her fantasy world was in her classroom and her great adventure was in opening the wondrous imaginations of her children.

• • •

Wynona was out the door and preparing to get in her car when she stopped, struck by the tranquility of the world she had entered. It was twilight. The sun set a little earlier in Brandstad due to the mountains to the west. The air was sweet with the smell of June's flower garden and the blooming crabapple trees in the front yard. It was a perfect early summer evening with a slight breeze that sighed softly through the trees. There was no traffic, no sound of sirens, no drone of aircraft engines overhead, nothing to break the peace. *Was it always like this?* she wondered. It was a short three blocks to Bill's, so Wynona decided to walk. As she did, she passed house after house that held memories for her. Maybe it was being exposed to the gentle-heartedness of her sister, or maybe it was just the soft-ness of a small town's summer evening, but Wynona began to relax inside just a little. She looked up and noticed the first evening stars becoming visible against the darkening sky. In the distance she heard the train that ran about a mile outside of town. She remembered so many summer nights when she would listen to the sound of the trains and wonder where they were going. She would imagine that they were headed off to the sea or sparkling cities or other fantastic places. Mostly she wished she was on them because she wanted to be somewhere, anywhere, but in Brandstad. All that seemed a distant memory to her now. She knew what it was like to be in a sparkling city, and she had learned that all that sparkles was not gold. Maybe she was missing the piece of her childhood that still could dream of someplace in this vast world where she belonged.

She turned the corner at Main Street, walked the last block to Bill's, and peered into the window. Wynona was not afraid of con-frontation, but this was going to be different. She was going to do something she rarely did—apologize. She strained her eyes to see if she could spot Brandon but was unable to see who was in the kitchen. Everything inside her said that she should turn around and just tell Beth that she had done it. But she knew Beth would know she was lying. Besides, she had promised, and breaking a promise was something that she and Beth never did to each other. *OK*, she thought, *I'll just go in there and say I'm sorry and get out, no big deal.* But it *was* a big deal because she knew this apology was far more than just being sorry for unkind words said; it was really about the cruel way she had treated Brandon eight years ago. There was another reason this was going to be difficult. The Brandon she had known in the past was handsome, but the Brandon she had seen that day in the restaurant was gorgeous. In the years since they had dated, he had developed a muscular physique, and he now carried himself with a confidence she had not seen before. Even the way he spoke to her in the diner was different. Things had changed for the better with Brandon, and Wynona was attracted to this improved version. Wynona caught herself in these thoughts and reminded herself that he was still working as a cook in a small-town diner; he was still going nowhere. She would never be happy with someone like that. That's why she had moved away, to get away from temptations like Brandon that would keep her stuck in Brandstad.

She took a deep breath, pushed open the glass door, and made her way to the lunch counter. The omnipresent Clara was there, busily helping customers, and she waved at Wynona as she shuffled between tables. Wynona craned her neck to look into the kitchen, but stacks of dishes blocked her view. She sat there for several minutes, getting more and more anxious and wishing she could get Clara's attention so she could go ask Brandon to come out. She had a sentence worked out and was rehearsing it under her breath: "Brandon, I was insensitive and unkind in what I said earlier, and I would like to apologize." As she said these words over and over again, she picked up a setting of silverware. She beat time with the spoon while attempting a balancing act with the fork and knife on the sugar dispenser. When Wynona was nervous, she started playing with anything within her reach. And she was very nervous. She was so focused on her little sugar dispenser project and rehearsing her apology that she failed to see Brandon come out of the kitchen and take the stool next to her.

"Apology accepted."

The sugar dispenser went flying into the air, as did the knife, spoon, and fork. Wynona was so unsettled that she nearly fell off her stool but managed to make it look like she was merely attempting to retrieve the fallen tableware.

"OK, then we're good?" Wynona said, hoping that she could flee the embarrassing moment without further damage to her ego.

"On one condition." Brandon turned toward her on his stool, and she looked for the first time into his deep blue eyes.

When did they get so blue? she thought. She didn't remember them being that blue.

"Condition?" she asked tentatively.

"Remember the three-thing rule?" Again he spoke, but her thoughts were now tangled in his eyes. *Who has eyes like that?*

Trying desperately to look away from Brandon's face and hoping to break the spell, she shook her head and managed to say, "Three-thing rule? What three-thing rule?"

"How could you forget? When one of us did something that was worthy of an apology, the other would get to ask them to do three things as a sort of penance."

Wynona pulled herself up to her full height. "I don't remember that. You made that up!"

"Then apology not accepted." Brandon stood up and began to walk back to the kitchen.

Wynona was in a predicament. She did not want to go back to Beth and tell her that Brandon had refused her apology, and yet she hated appearing weak to anyone by giving in. But there was another reason she didn't want this conversation to end this way. She was fascinated with this new Brandon and wanted to find out when and how he got this way.

"One! I will do one thing as long as it's not weird."

Brandon stopped at the end of the counter and turned toward Wynona. "Three or it's no deal."

If there was one thing Wynona had become good at, it was negotiations. She had pulled many deals out of the fire at work and could stare down even the most seasoned negotiator. She stood her ground. "No deal then."

"OK, no deal." Brandon turned to go back to the kitchen.

Wynona took a few steps toward the kitchen door, and just before Brandon disappeared behind it, she spoke. "Two and that's my final offer."

Brandon continued into the kitchen, and the door swung closed. Wynona stood for a moment, hoping that he would come out, but he did not emerge. After a few moments, she turned to leave, and just as she reached the end of the counter, the kitchen door swung open and Brandon strode confidently over to her.

"Deal. Meet me here tomorrow at five in the afternoon, and wear comfortable clothes." He turned back toward the kitchen.

"Remember—nothing too weird, right?" Wynona didn't like surprises, and it seemed as if she had just committed herself to a big one.

"Depends on your definition of weird." Brandon disappeared again behind the door, leaving Wynona to deal with the rare and uncomfortable feeling that she was not in control.

Back at home, Wynona recounted the scene to Beth, omitting the embarrassing parts like when she threw all the utensils on the floor. She asked Beth if she knew what was on Brandon's mind, but Beth said with a wink and a smile that it would be better for her to find out on her own. Wynona's times with Beth were brief but very, very deep. It seemed that as Beth's physical condition became weaker, her spirit grew stronger. She never had been one for small talk, but now the little speaking she did had a gravitas to it that was hard to describe. It was as if one was speaking to a Greek oracle because her words had great insight and power. Wynona found herself wishing she could record them. But that never seemed appropriate. However, she had found one of her old journals and began making entries after her conversations so that she would not forget what was spoken. Wynona did not realize it at the time, but in the few days she had been home, she was gradually becoming a different person. She found herself listening, not just to music, but to people, to birds, even to the wind. All the sounds she had generally ignored before, she was now awakened to. She also found herself feeling emotions that either she had suppressed or were simply absent from her normal world. These were not always pleasant feelings. She would look at a lovely sunset and begin to cry for no apparent reason. Or a smell would conjure up an emotion that she could not attach to any particular memory. It was as if Wynona had been in a long winter's hibernation and was now awakening. What was the cause of this? It could only be attributed to the love of her sister, Beth. Some people have that gift. They inspire beauty inside and out and challenge us to be more alive simply by our being exposed to them.

After Wynona's time with Beth, she had a small dinner with her mother and was pleasantly surprised that she wasn't completely bored by the conversation. In fact, it appeared that even June Swanson had made remarkable growth during Wynona's absence. Where was the idle-brained ninny that she remembered growing up with? Yes, there were still times when she cringed at June's naïve, politically incorrect comments and her complete failure to understand the nuanced sensibilities of the world outside of Brandstad, but by and large, Wynona's conversations with June were now pleasant and even affectionate.

After saying good night to her sister, Wynona retired to her bedroom to contemplate her day. She hoped to also get a restful night's sleep. The evening was warm and pleasant, so she opened wide her window and breathed in the sweet-smelling night air. As she lay on her bed, she once again heard the sound of the train in the distance as it drummed its rhythmic cadence across the village. Again, memories flooded into her, and she found herself wondering if the little girl who had lain in this bed dreaming night after night would be happy with the woman she had become. Yes, she had managed to escape the small town and its people and make herself a reasonable success in the city, but was that what she dreamed about so long ago? Didn't she dream about things like love, happiness, and friendship? Didn't she yearn to be liked and accepted? It wasn't until later, after so much rejection, that she stopped believing those things were attainable, and then she just wanted to escape. As her mind drifted back to her childhood, another yearning came over her, one that had been buried for years. She longed for her father. Warm tears began to roll down her cheeks as she remembered the giant of a man who would sweep her up into his arms and rub his rough cheeks lightly against hers. She remembered his smell, the musky aftershave he wore and the fragrance of outdoors that permeated his clothing. How she longed for him, and now she felt alone and scared, just like that little girl did the day he died. Then another feeling came over her, one that was very familiar—rage. Why did he die? What meaning did his death have? He was a volunteer firefighter who had been called out to work the Parker Woods fire, a forest fire of colossal proportions, burning more than five hundred thousand acres. He led a crew of hotshots who were specially trained to go into rugged terrain and attack the fire at its most vulnerable points. His crew had been caught in a sudden wind shift and had been overcome by the inferno. Five lives, including her father's, were extinguished that night. She had been taught that God was love, but what loving God would allow her father to be taken from her? Rage was the only emotion that Wynona allowed herself to feel for any length of time because when she was angry, she was not vulnerable, and if she was not vulnerable, she couldn't be hurt. What Wynona didn't understand was that it was this invulnerability that kept her from feeling love, receiving comfort, and healing from the devastating loss of her father.

It might seem somewhat understandable that she would have such animosity toward God, but what about the town? Why did she hate Brandstad? The source of this hatred was what Wynona saw as a failure on the part of the town to provide her father with adequate equipment to do his job—equipment that could have saved his and the other men's lives. Wynona had always been told that her father's death was an unavoidable accident. Tragic, yes, but one of the inherent risks of fighting forest fires. After all, who can predict sudden shifts in the wind? But Wynona was not satisfied with these pat answers. True to her nature, she did not rest until she had learned all she could about the events leading up to, and including, the night of his death. Wynona had barely turned twelve when she set out to reconstruct the events of the Parker Woods fire. She interviewed eyewitnesses, read the transcripts of the state inquest, and even examined the town council meeting minutes for a year prior to the fire. What she discovered was that the firemen were sent into the fire with inadequate communications equipment, and even though other crews had knowledge of the dangerous winds, they were unable to share this information with her father's crew. From the minutes of the city council meetings, Wynona discovered that the fire department had requested funding for radio equipment six months prior to the Parker Woods fire. The request had been approved, but then withdrawn and reallocated for remodeling the office of the newly elected sheriff, Joe Reilly. Of course, Sheriff Joe could not have known that this reallocation would indirectly lead to tragedy. In fact, the city council's action was unknown to him. But for Wynona, this was a smoking gun, and she was convinced that a price must be paid for such inexcusable incompetence. In her eyes, the entire city council was guilty of involuntary manslaughter, and she took it upon herself to press the issue until justice was done. She wrote editorials to the local newspaper, which were not published, and petitioned the state fire marshal to reopen the inquiry into her father's death, but to no avail. She even picketed city hall and called for the recall of the mayor and the sheriff. Eventually all that came of her efforts was a visit to her home from the school principal and the threat of suspension if she did not cease her vendetta. No one in the town had any interest in resurrecting the events of that fateful night. Even her mother was content to "let well enough alone" and move on with her life. Only Beth gave Wynona a sympathetic ear, and after hearing the evidence, she concluded that the city council had made a poor choice in remodeling an office instead of purchasing much-needed communications equipment. But Beth also wisely realized that there had been no malicious intent, and therefore she would not hold the decision against them. But Wynona would not forgive and would not forget, and it was clear that a great deal of her teenage rebelliousness was directly related to her belief that Brandstad had robbed her of her father.

Eventually Wynona fell into a restless sleep and dreamed the same dream she had had for more nights than she could number. This was more than a dream though; it was actually a memory of the last time she saw her father—although she no longer knew which part was dream and which part was memory. In her dream, she was a little girl about six years old, sleeping in her bedroom. Suddenly, she was awakened by the sound of sirens and movement downstairs. She rose and opened her bedroom door, then slowly walked to the top of the stairs. Looking down, she saw her father and mother at the front door. Her mother was helping her father put on his heavy fire jacket. She tried to call out to him not to go, but her voice didn't work. Then she attempted to run down the stairs to grab him and keep him from going, but she couldn't move her feet; she was paralyzed. Her panic increased as she stood at the top of the stairs, unable to keep her father from leaving. She watched as her parents embraced and her father put on his fireman's helmet. Her father opened the front door, and outside, Wynona could see a raging firestorm that engulfed her parents in a light so brilliant that she had to shut her eyes tightly. Knowing her father was about to go out into that fire, she forced open her eyes just in time to see him go out the door. Wynona knew he was never coming back. At this point in her dream, she would usually wake up sobbing. This time was no exception. Wynona woke with streams of hot tears on her cheeks, and her heart raced as if she had just sprinted a mile. How she hated that dream! It always made her feel so helpless. She looked over at the alarm clock and saw that it was 4:30 in the morning. She heard music coming from downstairs. It was impossible to go back to sleep, so she reluctantly pushed back the covers and went down to see who else was awake.

The music was quiet but distinct in the otherwise silent house. "And I say to myself, 'What a wonderful world...'" It was the classic Louis Armstrong recording, and it was coming from Beth's room. Her door was open a crack and Wynona looked in to see Beth with a flashlight in her hand, pointing it about the room as she quietly sang along with Satchmo. Here she was, dying a slow, painful death, and she was singing about a wonderful world. Wynona pushed open the door a bit more to see that the flashlight was throwing out tiny pin-points of light upon the ceiling and walls. The lights looked like stars. Beth adjusted the light, and it projected a vibrant constellation with many swirling colors. It was amazingly beautiful, and Wynona stood mesmerized. Still feeling the effects of her vivid nightmare, Wynona wondered if she had stepped into another dream. But this one was wonderful and somehow healing. She didn't know how long she had been standing entranced in the doorway when Beth noticed her.

"Come on in, Sis, and enjoy the lightshow." Wynona stepped farther into Beth's room, and could see the full effect of what she now realized was a laser show. The song ended, and Beth turned off the laser device and flipped a switch next to her pillow that turned on the bedside lamp. "You're up awfully early. How are you sleeping?"

Wynona sat down next to Beth. "Who's talking? What's with the early morning concert and light show?"

"The meds make me sleep when I should be awake and awake when I should be sleeping. Besides, this thing that my kids gave me works best when it's totally dark." Beth held up the laser.

Wynona took it and looked it over. "Pretty nice."

"Yeah, they know how much I love the stars, so they thought it might cheer me up to see them on my ceiling...They were right. Isn't the universe wonderful?"

"So you say," Wynona said coolly.

"What's up, Sis? Are you worried about me? If so, you shouldn't be. You know that I'm not afraid of dying. In fact, I'm looking forward to the next great adventure."

"Who's to say that it gets better? Maybe it's worse." Wynona was still half asleep; otherwise she would never have entered into a serious conversation about death with her sister.

Beth looked hard at Wynona and noticed the effect of her nightmare still evident on her face. "See that butterfly there?"

Wynona realized that she was entering a topic she abhorred, especially with someone who was a fanatical Christian like Beth. "Which one? They're everywhere. This room is one big butterfly farm."

"I like butterflies. Do you know why?" Beth let her eyes wander about the room, gazing with joy at all the different butterflies her kids had made for her.

Knowing that she had to engage in this discussion but hoping that she could get out of it quickly, Wynona responded, "I don't know. Because they're pretty?"

Beth, with a twinkle in her eyes, turned again to Wynona. "Yes, they are that, so very beautiful. But the biggest reason is because they go through a metamorphosis. Do you know what that is?"

Now Wynona went from feeling annoyed with the topic to feeling like she was in Beth's second-grade class. But she was determined not to be unkind; after all, this was her very ill sister she was talking to. "Yes, Beth, I know what metamorphosis means."

"Caterpillar to butterfly...caterpillar to butterfly." Once again, Beth's energy appeared to suddenly leave her like a cloud passing over the sun. She repeated the phrase a few more times, and then she was off into a deep sleep. Wynona was not accustomed to these quick departures and sat for a few moments expecting Beth to finish her thought, but then she realized this was the end of the conversation. She felt both relieved and strangely disappointed that Beth hadn't finished explaining her mysterious fascination with butterflies. In the end, Wynona reasoned that it was a conversation she should have avoided anyway. She pulled the covers up over Beth, placed the laser device on the nightstand, and left the room.

The day was just beginning and the night shadows slowly faded with the growing light in the east. It was another day in Brandstad, and all Wynona had to look forward to was a date with Brandon, doing something she was certain she would not like. For the majority of the day, Wynona worked from the house on her laptop, trying to get a head start on the pile of work that was sure to be waiting for her when she returned to the office. She also took frequent breaks for short conversations with Beth. The topic of butterflies did not come up again. This was either because Beth did not remember the previous conversation or because Wynona intentionally avoided it, which was more likely. When it came time to leave for Bill's, Wynona changed into something she thought might be appropriate for the evening. And much to her surprise, she also took care to look attractive, though she hardly knew why she would do that.

11
The LARPers Make a Plan

"I JUST THINK it's not normal for her to dress like that," said Fred Summerville as he passed the vegetables to his wife.

"Leave her alone. At least she's not on drugs or doing God knows what she was doing at college." Susan Summerville took a spoonful of vegetables and put the dish down on the table.

"And what is she doing out in the forest with those freaks? I tell you that's just not normal." Fred cut a piece of meat and stuck it in his mouth. "So where is she? It's six o'clock, and we always eat at six o'clock."

Susan put down her fork, picked up a small bell on the table, and rang it. Sara, a rather portly elderly woman in a maid's dress, stepped in from the adjoining kitchen. "Sara, would you please find Lisa and tell her to come to dinner?" Sara looked at her mistress with incredulity. Susan glared back and exclaimed, "Don't give me that look. Just go and tell her."

Sara walked out of the room, muttering, "You know she don't mind me. I'll tell her, but if the child don't want to come, she won't come." Sara shuffled through the parlor and then came to the entryway of the large Victorian house that had been built around the turn of the century. It was situated at the highest point in Brandstad as a testament to the power of the family that lived there. She peered up the long winding stairway and stopped. She wondered if she should bother climbing the stairs to deliver the message. Then she stepped back and let out what could only be described as a holler: *"Lisa! Lisa!"*

From the top of the stairs, Lisa popped her head over the banister. "What?"

"Dinner is served. Get your bony butt down here!" Sara spoke with an authority born out of a position of familiarity that was far more than a household servant. Sara had been with the family since Lisa was a child and during that time had been more of a mother to her than her own. Sara loved Lisa, and the feeling was mutual.

"What'd you cook?" Still only Lisa's head was visible as she looked down from the railing.

"What's it matter what I cooked? Everything I cook is delicious! So you get yourself down here, and don't make me haul this tired body up there to fetch you down."

"OK, I'm coming." There was a bit of a commotion, and then a slender green-and-blue body came sliding down the banister, finishing at the bottom with a flip that almost knocked over Sara.

Sara dodged Lisa and shouted, "Child, this ain't no circus. You're going to kill someone."

Lisa gave Sara an affectionate hug and whispered in her ear, "Don't worry. I'd never kill you, Sara, but I won't make any promises about the other people in this house." Lisa then headed off to the dining room.

Sara shook her head as she watched her leave. "Honey, sometimes you scare me to death."

In the dining room, Lisa sat in her chair and picked through the various foods that were laid out. She put a few morsels on her plate, poured herself a large glass of water, and began to eat. Susan looked over at her daughter's selections and said, "You're not eating enough to—"

Lisa threw up one hand in the direction of her mother and shouted, "Stop!" Susan stopped in midsentence. "If you're going to comment on what I eat, how much I eat, when I eat, or anything else about eating, then I will take my food to my room and eat what I like, how much I like, and when I like."

Susan looked over at Fred. "Well, say something."

Fred, without a pause in putting food in his mouth, said, "She's got a point. I think what she eats is her business." He turned to his daughter. "But I think you could speak to your mother in a more civil way."

Lisa gave him a matter-of-fact look and with no emotion said, "Tried that. Doesn't work."

Obviously flustered, Susan was mumbling something about appreciation or respect when the doorbell rang. "Oh, that's for me." Lisa jumped up from her chair and bolted toward the front door.

"Wait a second, young lady." Fred could use a commanding voice when he wanted to, and here, he wanted to. "Who is at the door?"

Lisa turned toward her father and said, "Friends."

"What friends?" he responded.

"My friends," she said, avoiding his question.

Fred rose to his feet and walked over to Lisa. "Are these the freakish friends you go into the woods with?"

"They are not freaks, and yes, we go into the woods. Hiking in the woods is healthy. My therapist said so."

"Normal people hike in the woods; freaks dress up like comic-book characters and do God knows what in the woods."

Maybe because she felt unsupported by her husband or maybe because she really believed that Lisa's excursions into the forest were healthier than the other things she had done, Susan rose to Lisa's defense. "Fred, I think you shouldn't be so critical of Lisa's friends. They're good kids."

"How do we know they're not sacrificing chickens or doing some other weird occult stuff?" Fred was reaching, but he hated what he did not understand, and LARPing was something he could not understand.

"Really, Dad? Is that what you think? Really?" Lisa turned and walked out of the room.

Fred watched her leave and then turned to his wife. Susan smirked at her husband and took some pleasure in seeing him so badly overplay his hand with his daughter. "Really, Fred, you must stop overreacting."

"Come with me, and tell me if I'm overreacting." Fred put his hand on the small of her back and pushed his wife through the doorway and toward the entry hall. Sara had already opened the door and allowed Connor and Kyle to come in. The Summervilles saw a fully arrayed warrior and a dwarf, who were then joined by Lori, an elf. Fred and Susan stood several paces from the group, and Fred exclaimed to his wife, "Do you think I'm overreacting now?"

Susan was damned if she was going to let her husband get the last word, so she strolled right up to Kyle as if he were an honored guest at one of her cocktail parties. "Hello, I'm Susan Summerville, Lisa's mother, and you are?" She reached out to shake Kyle's hand, which was troublesome on two counts. First, because Kyle was extremely awkward in any social situation, and second because he was wearing large leather gloves that were more suited to welding than hand shaking.

Kyle fumbled to remove a glove and ended up dropping it. As he stooped to pick it up, his iron helmet fell with a crash on the beautiful parquet floor.

Lisa moaned. "This is all I need."

But to Kyle's credit, he still managed to somehow get an arm extended in the direction of Mrs. Summerville. "I am Kyle...I mean...I am Brummel the Dwarf."

"Oh, I have never met a dwarf before. It's so good to make your acquaintance." At this point, it was impossible to know whether Susan was sincere or if she was mocking Kyle. She had become an expert at faking sincerity in so many social situations that she was superb at camouflaging her contempt. "And you are?" she asked as she extended her hand to Connor.

"Connor Reilly, Mrs. Summerville." He made an awkward bowing gesture before grabbing her hand and pumping it violently.

"Oh, Connor, yes, I am sorry. I didn't recognize you in this handsome outfit." Susan then added to her mocked politeness a well-honed flirting as she ran her finger down Connor's exposed bicep. "And who are you dressed up to be?"

"Perales the Proud, ma'am. I'm a warrior."

Looking at Connor admiringly, she said, "Yes, you are."

Fred couldn't stand it any longer. "So, Connor, does your father approve of what you're doing?"

"Well, he doesn't exactly approve, but he says as long as we're not smoking something or doing anything too weird, he's OK with it."

"There, you see? If the sheriff doesn't mind, then who are we to criticize? So, Lisa, would you and your friends like some dessert? I think we're having Baked Alaska tonight. Isn't that right, Sara?" But when Susan turned to Sara, she saw that she was so taken by the sight of Kyle and Connor in all their LARP splendor that all she could do was nod her head.

Lisa could see that this was not going the way she had planned, so she began to move the group out of the entryway and toward the door to the basement. "Maybe later, Mom. We've got business to do first." Kyle and Connor disappeared down the steps as Lisa closed the door.

The Summervilles' basement was finished, like everything else in their home, ostentatiously. There was a marble floor and dark wood paneling, with a large wet bar at one end. Connor reached the bottom of the stairs and whined, "Hey, why the rush? I would have liked dessert. I'm hungry."

"You're always hungry. Besides, you don't even know what Baked Alaska is." Lisa flipped on some overhead lights that accented the assortment of oil paintings and stuffed animals that adorned the walls of the basement. "Let's get to work."

Still disappointed, Connor replied, "What work?"

"Kyle, you're the LARP expert here. What do we do now that we don't have a wizard?"

Kyle had been completely unprepared for his opulent surroundings. His eyes darted from picture to stuffed animal to the almost life-sized statue of a cowboy in the corner.

"Kyle, are you with us?" Lisa waved her hand in front of Kyle's face. "What do we do without a wizard?"

"Well, we certainly will find it hard to compete without a wizard because all the other fellowships have one."

There was a pause, and Lisa stared impatiently. "So?"

Kyle didn't like to be questioned. It made him nervous, and when he got nervous, he got tongue-tied. "So...We need a wizard."

While Lisa and Kyle talked, Connor found his way to the bar. "I'm more interested in getting even with the one we have now. He can't ditch us and get away with it. Besides, that dragon is mine."

"Don't be an idiot. Brandon is the best wizard we're going to find around here, and if we ever want to win a contest, we need to get him back." Lisa walked over to the bar, grabbed a bottle of scotch from Brandon's hand and put it back on the shelf. "Thirty-year-old single malt is wasted on you...Grab a beer from the fridge." Connor shrugged and complied.

Kyle muttered, "Can we do both?"

"What?"

"If we find the dragon, or whatever it is, before Brandon, we'll get all the experience points, and then he'll have to come back."

Connor popped the lid on a beer and exclaimed, "Freakin' brilliant. You're a freakin' brilliant little man." He walked over and ruffled Kyle's shaggy red hair. "I take the dragon from the wizard, and he's left with nothing, so he has to come back with his little wizard tail between his little wizard legs."

"OK, I like it!" Lisa exclaimed. "But one thing I have to know for sure before we start combing through the woods—what the hell are we looking for?"

"I told you. Nobody knows. All we know is that it's big and it's cavernous."

Kyle muttered, "Carnivorous."

Connor took another swig of his beer. "What?"

Lisa could see that Connor would not take well to being corrected by Kyle, so she interjected. "The word is *carnivorous*. It means it eats meat."

"Yeah, that's what I said...cavernous. There were bones and skulls all around its cage, and its tracks were this big." Connor made a motion with his hands, one still holding his beer, of about three feet across.

Kyle was just beginning to see the major flaw in his plan. "We're going to go looking for that?"

"Nope, that thing will come looking for us, and we'll be ready." Connor then unsheathed his sword and began going through the sword-wielding routine that they had all seen a million times.

Kyle took a step back from Connor. He didn't trust his swordplay, especially when he was drinking. "I don't like the idea of being in the forest with something that big that eats people."

"Relax, little man. I'm here. I'll kill the big, bad dragon before it eats you." Connor made a quick move with his sword; it slipped from his hand, flew across the room, and impaled a couch cushion.

"I'm dead," Kyle whispered to himself.

"So where do we start looking?" Lisa asked as she motioned for the group to huddle in the middle of the room.

Retrieving his sword, Connor said, "My dad said that it went into the forest just east of Old Man Stealy's house, so that is where we should start."

Lisa put her hand into the center of the trio. "So we meet at Bill's Friday morning at seven, and we'll drive to Old Man Stealy's house and begin our quest to find the dragon."

Kyle shifted awkwardly and mumbled, "Sorry, I've got to work. Could we begin the quest on Saturday?"

Lisa sighed and revised her declaration. "OK, we meet at Bill's on Saturday and then drive to Old Man Stealy's house and begin our quest to find the dragon." The others placed their hands on top of hers and repeated, as they had rehearsed on their other quests: "We quest to find the dragon."

And Connor added, "And kill it."

• • •

Willy, a young police intern, was sitting behind the counter as Sheriff Joe walked in. Willy reluctantly gave the sheriff news he knew would not be well received. "Sheriff, the mayor is waiting for you."

Sheriff Joe and Mayor Lindquist had a contentious relationship. The sheriff was single-minded in one pursuit of his office—to keep the peace and order of Brandstad—while the mayor was just as single-minded in his quest to fulfill every expectation of every voter. These pursuits didn't often clash, but when they did, it was like the proverbial irresistible force against an immovable object.

"Damn. What does he want?"

"Well, I can't be certain, but there's been a lot of crazy talk about whatever escaped from Old Man Stealy's place. He's talkin' about getting a posse together."

"That's all I need, a bunch of idiots running about in the woods with pitchforks."

Sheriff Joe pushed past the reception desk into a larger room of desks until he was greeted by his secretary, who sat just outside his office.

"Is he—"

"'Fraid so, Sheriff."

Sheriff Joe sighed. "Dammit."

He entered his office and closed the door. The office staff found reasons to linger about. They couldn't make out the entire conversation, but they did overhear the gist of it. The sheriff's speech was slow but determined, and Mayor Lindquist's voice could be heard in an excited, high-pitched semiscream. The door suddenly burst open, and out came a stern Sheriff Joe ignoring a scattering office staff. Sheriff Joe walked past various city offices until he came to the animal control office. He opened the door to see Steve and Henry lounging. Steve was eating a large sandwich and had a tray of sticky buns in front of him; his feet were propped up on his desk. Henry's attention was fully engaged in a video game.

Looking up from his sandwich, Steve asked, "To what do we owe this pleasure, Sheriff?"

Sheriff Joe walked into the office and sauntered around the room, looking at various things, until he stood next to Henry, who was still frantically fighting off space aliens with his joystick.

Sheriff Joe gave Henry a thin smile. "Winning?"

"I'm on the tenth level...my personal best."

"Glad to hear it." He walked over to Steve, who was still busy devouring his sandwich.

"Good sandwich?"

Steve grunted affirmatively.

"From Bill's, right?"

Steve grunted again.

"Yep, they make a mighty fine sandwich at Bill's." Then, with one swift move, he tossed Steve's feet off the desk, swiveled his chair so that they were eye to eye, and glared intensely at Steve. "I have just one question for you, Mr. Animal-Control Expert. Are you being paid to sit on your butt stuffing your face, or are you doing what's painted on that door?"

Steve, trying desperately to swallow the large piece of sandwich he had just put in his mouth, was only able to say, "What door?"

The sheriff walked over to the door and opened it. The words stenciled on the glass read "Animal Control." Turning back to the twosome, his temper seething, he grabbed the arms of Steve's chair. "Seems to me that we've got some kind of animal in the woods that is out of control, and I want it under control. Do you hear me?"

Steve was finally able to swallow the food that was stuck in his throat and croaked out, "But, Sheriff, we've been busy collecting the other animals from the Stealy house."

Looking at Henry, the sheriff asked, "So how's that going?"

"Pretty good."

"OK, so you've got those animals under control. Now finish the job before I make a phone call to your boss and tell him what a pair of knuckleheads you are and get your fat asses kicked out of my city."

Steve attempted to protest but didn't get more than two words out of his mouth before Sheriff Joe shut it for him. "You can't—"

"I can't what?"

Thinking better of his statement, Steve retreated to a peace offering. "You can't leave without taking one of Bill's sticky buns. They're the best." Steve pushed the trayful of gooey buns toward Sheriff Joe. The sheriff took the tray and walked slowly to the door. Steve and Henry breathed a sigh of relief, thinking they had weathered the storm, when he suddenly turned and squished the entire tray of buns against the lettering on the door. "Now get your lazy carcasses out there and find that thing, whatever it is!"

Sheriff Joe turned and exited down the hall while Steve and Henry slowly rose and walked sheepishly to the door. Henry wiped the perspiration off his brow. "That was close."

Steve looked down the hallway to make sure Sheriff Joe was gone and then turned back to the door where the mushy mass of pastry had slid to the floor. "What a shame."

Henry, still looking down the hall, said, "Yeah, he had no right to do that to perfectly good sticky buns." He slid his finger across the door and put it into his mouth.

12
The Date

THE MORNING WAS a never-ending stream of well-wishers coming to see Beth. They filed into her room for an audience as if she were the pope. At one point, Wynona counted four people sitting in the living room waiting. The hospice nurse was transformed into an appointment secretary, who made sure that each supplicant had only the time that Beth's strength would allow. Wynona had dedicated the day to catching up on work via her laptop but found that the interruptions were too frequent, and she could not spend any quality time concentrating on her work. This was really the first time that Wynona had felt the full weight of Beth's influence on the community. Among the visitors were fellow teachers, old school friends, and friends from church. Wynona had no idea how some of the other visitors knew Beth.

Two visitors stood out. Kyle came during his lunch break and brought a few wilted flowers arranged in a vase. They looked like he had plucked them out of the recycling bin. Wynona asked herself, "How the hell does Beth know him?" Wynona was so curious that she couldn't resist eavesdropping on their conversation. What she heard was mostly Beth talking to a silent Kyle. She opened the door a bit more and was able to see him. He had tears running down his cheeks as Beth spoke. Beth received the pitiful little vase of flowers as if it were two dozen roses and gushed with appreciation. It was all Kyle could do to lift his head and look at Beth. He was so stricken with grief. Finally, the nurse came in to tell him his time was up, and Beth reached out to take his hand. Kyle clumsily grabbed her hand and kissed it—not like the movie stars do in historical dramas, but more like a person who is overcome with love and doesn't know how else to express it. Wynona was moved by this simple demonstration of affection.

The other unexpected guest was Lisa. Wynona did not listen in on that conversation, but when Lisa left, it was clear that she too was affected by being in the presence of Beth. This was the case over and over again with all who entered into the hallowed space where Beth was. Everyone loved Beth, but it was more than love that brought them to her bedside. Beth gave them something they needed. Something that Wynona could not yet understand.

Later in the afternoon, after the nurse had ushered the waiting visitors from the house with the announcement that Beth needed her sleep, Wynona had her own brief visit. Beth was happy to hear that she was going to see Brandon, and she was also pleased that the house would be quiet so that she could get some rest.

As Wynona stepped out of the house, she noticed a little sign the nurse had put on the door: "Please, no more visitors today. Beth is sleeping." The sign had hand-drawn butterflies. It was another beautiful afternoon, so Wynona decided she would again walk the several blocks to Bill's. As she strolled the picturesque sidewalks of Brandstad, she thought to herself how it was funny she didn't remember the small village being so lovely. She only remembered the frigid winters and the oppressively hot, mosquito-infested summers.

She arrived at Bill's a few minutes after five and sat at the counter to wait for Brandon. He strolled out a few minutes later, wiping off his hands with a towel. "So you did come," he said with a bit of surprise in his voice.

"I always keep my promises."

Brandon leaned over the counter and looked hard at her. "Is that right?"

"Well, at least the promises I *can* keep." She matched his gaze with one of her own.

"Good, then; let's go. My car is out front." He walked around the counter and headed for the door.

Wynona swiveled around on the barstool. "Go where?"

"You'll find out." And then Brandon was out the door and climbing into what appeared to be a World War II—era Jeep.

She heaved a big sigh, ran out of Bill's, and took her position in the passenger seat. Brandon cranked up the engine, and they were off. The wind was barely obstructed by the small windshield as they flew down Main Street to the county road turnoff. Wynona couldn't help but feel exhilarated by the ride, but she was also a bit alarmed because she soon realized that the only thing keeping her from being pitched out of the antique vehicle was a very crude seatbelt that was probably installed over sixty years ago. She cinched up the belt as tightly as she could and held onto whatever seemed more stable than she was. Occasionally, she would glance over at Brandon and see him grinning with joy. She wondered if that was because he was going to enjoy the adventure or because he knew that she was not going to. She still held the fear that all this was an elaborate subterfuge to get even with her for the way she left Brandstad and him eight years ago. But she didn't need to fear. Brandon was a man who had learned to let go of resentment and grab hold of his bliss, and he was on his way to introducing her to his major bliss. After several miles, Brandon turned at a small paved road, and soon they arrived at a building with a sign on the front that said, "Summerville Animal Shelter."

Wynona read the sign. "Summerville?"

"Give unto Caesar that which is Caesar's. Mr. Summerville gave most of the money, and we gave him his name on the building." Brandon leaped from the Jeep and started up the front walkway. "It was the dream of many of us a few years ago to have a place where abandoned domestic and wounded animals could be cared for. We are now celebrating our third year in operation." He pushed open the door and entered a brightly lit reception room where an older gentleman sat at a desk.

"Hello, Paul. This is Wynona. She's here to help me tonight."

Paul looked up from his work and smiled. "Wynona—you're Beth's sister, right?"

"Yeah, and she's actually my sister, too." What Wynona said came out a bit snarky, but she was at the end of her tolerance when it came to being overshadowed by her sister. Paul just smiled back at her. Apparently the kindhearted man didn't even notice the rudeness of Wynona's comment. Brandon determined the less conversation, the better, so he hurried Wynona through the doors to the animal enclosures.

"This is the side where we keep all our domestic animals," Brandon said, pointing to the large cages full of various cats and dogs. "We got a large influx of animals a few days ago from Mr. Stealy's ranch, and we're still trying to process them." Wynona bent down at one cage that held an especially beautiful, big yellow dog. Brandon knelt down beside her.

"So you've met Clifton. He's special. He's been trained as a service dog, and we're looking for just the right person to match his skills."

Clifton continued to lick Wynona's fingers. "So we're here to keep them company and play with them, right?"

"Not exactly. First, we need to clean up." Brandon opened a closet and began rummaging about.

"You mean give them baths, right?"

Brandon found what he was looking for and handed Wynona a shovel. "Some of them. But first, we scoop poop."

Wynona looked incredulously at the shovel. "You drove me out here to shovel poop?" She looked around and saw that most of the dogs were small, and the cats all had litter boxes. She thought, *So how hard could it be?* Brandon turned and began to walk down the corridor, where there was another door at the far end. Wynona followed until they came to another, larger, enclosure where there were horses, a few sheep, and what appeared to be a full-grown bull.

Brandon stopped. "This is where the shovels come in handy." For all of Wynona's obstinacy, she did pitch in wholeheartedly with the work. She actually found it relaxing after the last few days of focusing on Beth and trying to cope with her reentrance into Brandstad. What she enjoyed most of all was Brandon's love for the animals and the cause he had committed himself to. He seemed to draw energy from the animals, and they in turn seemed to have a special appreciation for him. Wynona and Brandon worked their way through the large domestic animals and then went to feed and care for those that were not domesticated. Here she saw an assortment of animals, all in various stages of healing. Brandon patiently answered all of Wynona's questions about each and every animal they encountered. He told her the shelter was set up so that no animal that could be saved would ever be euthanized. The local veterinarians donated their time, but what they really needed was a full-time vet because Summerville was the only full-service shelter in this portion of the state, and the influx of needy animals was becoming overwhelming.

Wynona and Brandon ended up where they began, and at last, Wynona had a chance to revisit the little dogs she had met when she arrived. It had taken several hours to do their work, and Brandon went in to the employees' fridge and pulled out a couple of frosty sodas. They sat in the small-dog cage and laughed as the puppies jumped up on them and licked their faces, or anything else they could get their tongues on. Wynona couldn't stand the mystery of Brandon's transformation any longer. She put down an especially adorable puppy and asked, "So what happened to you?"

Brandon took a drink and wiped his face. "What do you mean?"

"What happened? You were never like this when we were dating."

"How do you know what I was like? You were too caught up in being unhappy to even notice who I was." This was the first indication of the hurt that Brandon had felt, but even now, he still didn't say it in a way that was the least bit spiteful.

"You seem...happy?" Wynona was surprised when she said this because she never thought in terms of happy and unhappy, only successful and unsuccessful.

"Wynona, I'm still a cook at Bill's, remember? But I do believe that I'm on the right path. Somehow, if I can just keep moving forward, I know there's something great ahead." Wynona didn't answer him right away. She played with the puppies, giving an occasional glance in his direction, and then words came out of her mouth that she could hardly believe. "Do you think I'm on the right path?"

Brandon didn't flinch. He was accustomed to asking self-examining questions and therefore did not balk when faced with hers. "What do you think?"

Wynona's face flushed with embarrassment. She felt like she were a little girl, and the teacher had called on her in front of the class to answer a question she should have known the answer to, but didn't. But she was fast on her feet and very good at deflection, so her survival skills kicked in. "I think it's time to exchange these sodas for something with a bit more kick. Is the Tree Hugger still open?" This was a restaurant and bar where the locals would go and the only place in town with live music, locally brewed beer, and pool tables.

"Haven't closed it yet, but Sheriff Joe keeps threatening to." Brandon knew that Wynona had reached her limit of self-disclosure, so he was happy to move the conversation to another topic and the venue to a different location.

Wynona picked herself up off the floor. "My treat."

The Tree Hugger was only a mile out of town and next to the river. It was frequented by everyone in town. It had been constructed with whole logs, which gave it a rustic look. The great room, with its high-beamed ceiling, led out to a large deck overhanging a portion of the river. At one end of the great room was a stage where a band played almost every night. The Tree Hugger was known for attracting quality bands that would perform just because it was such a unique venue and there was always an appreciative audience. Things were usually well ordered—with only an occasional fistfight prompted by a broken heart set free from its constraints by alcohol. And that was about as bad as it got at the Tree Hugger, until the periodic visit by some motorcycle gang that thought being in a small town meant they could act big. The regulars at the Tree Hugger were men who climbed one-hundred-foot trees and hauled two-ton logs for a living, which was one of the most dangerous professions on the planet. So when some leather-clad, tattooed motorcycle jocks came into town and abused the privilege of local hospitality, like insulting the beer, the music, or the women, there was always a price to pay. More than once, the motorcycle gangs had left Brandstad considerably less comfortable than when they arrived.

Brandon and Wynona found a parking place along the road because the lot was full. Brandon looked at the brightly lit building. "Must be a good band tonight. The place is packed."

Wynona was already out of the Jeep and walking toward the bar. "That's the way I like it!" Inside, the band was playing a Cajun style of music that was easy to listen to and easier to dance to. Wynona stepped into the building. "This I remember!" They found a table on the deck and ordered their first round of the special Tree Hugger lager. When she saw it on the menu, she said to Brandon, "Do you suppose anybody else sees the irony of calling the beer here a lager?" The moon was just rising from behind the mountains, and its reflection bounced off the ripples of the river in silvery flashes of blue light.

"Thank you for this evening. I had fun." Wynona was relaxing and beginning to let down the well-maintained protective wall that she had had for as long as she could remember.

Brandon smiled. "I was a bit worried when I handed you the shovel, but I must admit, you pitched right in."

Wynona replied, "Who would have thought that a bull could produce so much? I guess they don't call it bullshit for nothing." Just then, the band struck up an especially danceable piece, and Wynona jumped up from her seat. "Let's dance," she said. Brandon led her out onto the floor, and they began to do the two-step by following the other dancers in a large clockwise rotation around the floor. It had been years since Wynona had danced like this. The only occasions that required dancing these days were stuffy business meetings where the goal was to get the account, not kick up your heels on the dance floor. All the old steps were coming back to her, and she was totally immersed in the joy of dancing when Brandon suddenly lurched toward her and knocked her back into another couple. She looked to see what had caused him to stumble. It was Connor dancing with Lisa, and he had intentionally bumped into Brandon. Brandon composed himself and continued to dance until the song was over, and they returned to their table.

Wynona leaned across the table. "I take it Connor and you have a problem."

"Not my problem. It's his." Just then Connor appeared at their table and hovered over Brandon like a bird of prey.

"You still plan on finding the dragon without us?" Connor asked menacingly.

Brandon picked up his beer and took a drink. "You still plan on killing it when you find it?"

Connor shot back, "Without mercy."

He put down his beer and stood up. "Then I am going to find it without you." Connor took a step toward Brandon, and there would have been a real altercation if Lisa hadn't stepped in between them.

"Now, boys, let's not do anything rash. We'll just have to agree to disagree. May the best LARPer win, right?" Lisa turned to Connor and gave him a kiss on the cheek, which served to distract and relax him somewhat.

Connor then went into his cocky mode. "OK, then. I'll save you a tooth. I hear you wizards can do great things with a dragon's tooth." Brandon didn't reply, but his look said exactly what he thought of

Connor. Lisa saw that this was becoming way too intense. She wanted to preserve some hope of getting Brandon back into their LARP fellowship, so she attempted to change the subject by turning to Wynona.

"Wynona, I am very sorry about your sister. She's the sweetest person I know. If there's anything I or my family can do, please let me know."

Wynona looked up at Lisa, still feeling the unreality of two grown men about to break out in a fistfight over a dragon. "Thank you. That's kind of you." And with that, Connor and Lisa melted back into the Tree Hugger crowd, and Brandon sat back down at the table and took another sip of his beer.

Wynona gave Brandon a confused look. "You almost fought that guy...over a dragon."

Brandon took another sip of his beer. "Yep."

Wynona shook her head. "Has anyone ever told you that you're freakin' crazy?"

"I think you mentioned that several times a few years back." Brandon gave Wynona one of his patented "I don't give a damn" smiles.

"Just when I thought you'd changed, you do something like this. What is wrong with you?" Brandon didn't respond to Wynona's intensity. He simply leaned back in his chair and continued to sip his beer.

"So, you still owe me one more."

"What?"

"You owe me one more favor, remember?" At this point, Wynona was just trying to get her head around the case of mass schizophrenia she had witnessed and was in no mood to consider another date with Brandon.

Brandon put down his beer and leaned toward Wynona. "I am going to look for the dragon, so I want you to meet me at six in the morning at Old Man Stealy's house on Friday. Dress LARP style and be prepared for a very long hike."

Wynona could barely believe her ears. This crazy guy was asking her to go out and search for a dragon. "If I did that, I'd be as crazy as you and the rest of those freaks. Frankly, I enjoy my sanity."

"So you always keep your promises, huh?"

"Don't go there, Brandon. You know that there is no such thing as wizards, elves, dwarves, or dragons. I am a realist; I am happy to live in the real world."

"Are you? Are you happy in this real world? There are more things in heaven and earth than are dreamt of in your philosophy, Wynona."

"Shakespeare will not get me to believe in dragons." Wynona had had enough and was again fully confident in the reason she needed to leave Brandstad. It was this kind of stupidity that she had to escape. "I want you to take me home now." She got up and began to leave.

Brandon spoke up. "Aren't you forgetting something?" Wynona shot a killer look at him. "You said it was your treat." Wynona marched back to the table, threw a twenty on it, and marched toward the Jeep. The ride back was silent, and as Brandon pulled up into the driveway, he leaned over to Wynona. She recoiled, thinking he was looking for a kiss.

"Remember—Friday at six. Old Man Stealy's house. Dress appropriately. I think it might get rough."

Wynona could hardly be colder when she leaned into Brandon and said, "In your dreams." She then ejected herself from the Jeep and entered into the quiet but unsettling world of the Swanson home. Wynona couldn't have guessed that what she said to Brandon was true. Wynona dreamed a great many things that night. She dreamed of butterflies, dragons, wizards, and herself as a little girl. Her entire night was so filled with dreams that when she woke, she could hardly tell if she was still dreaming. It seemed everything inside of Wynona was being stirred and shaken. Her sister was dying, her old boyfriend was dressing up like some kind of nut and hunting dragons, and she was feeling like she was inescapably in the middle of the whole awful nightmare. In fact, she felt like her two feet were firmly planted in midair, and she was helpless to do anything but wait and hope that she could somehow get back to her normal life. But for Wynona, things would get more bizarre before they got better.

13

There's a Dragon in the Woods

IT WAS TWO days after the discovery of the bizarre scene at Old Man Stealy's house, and Steve and Henry had been busy collecting all the animals they had found and delivering them to the shelter. Neither of them spoke of it, but they both knew they would soon have to address the mystery of the dragon. They would have been happy to do nothing about it, but word had spread that something dangerous had escaped into the woods, and the talk in the town was turning increasingly paranoid. One hiker even claimed to have seen a huge creature with long fangs devouring a deer carcass, and others said that things were just not normal in the woods around Old Man Stealy's house, but they couldn't quite put their finger on what was wrong. Because of the persistence of these stories, people's imaginations began to run riot over their common sense, and the dread of some evil creature lurking in the forest grew. Even with all the rumors, Steve and Henry would have found a way to avoid any serious search if it had not been for Sheriff Joe coming to their office and telling them, in no uncertain terms, to get off their butts and into the woods. So, reluctantly, the duo set out to solve the mystery of the tracks going into the forest. Thursday morning found them parked next to the Stealy house, arguing about what they would need for their mission. Henry pleaded with Steve. "I tell you. We need something bigger than nets to go after whatever is in that forest."

"What would you suggest?" Steve opened the door of the truck to circle around to where they kept their equipment. "Maybe we should bring a bazooka?"

"We don't have one of those, but if we did, I would bring it." Henry joined Steve at the back of the truck.

"Then what?" Steve opened the back of the truck to reveal an assortment of animal-catching gear.

Henry pointed to a rifle fastened to a shelf. "Let's at least bring the tranquilizer gun."

Steve looked at Henry and shrugged his shoulders. "OK, bring it. But if we need to use it, I'm going to be the one to fire it. You're bound to shoot me before you'd hit an animal."

The two loaded up on the essential tools even though they had no idea what kind of animal they were looking for. They weren't even sure that there *was* an animal on the loose. Steve led the way, and Henry trailed behind, carrying most of the equipment. Anyone watching them would have thought they had stepped out of a Laurel and Hardy movie as they stumbled and bumbled their way through the woods, attempting to pick up the tracks of the fugitive creature. Stealy's house was situated on a high spot in the terrain, and behind the house was a slow and gentle slope that led down to a small stream. Steve and Henry followed the slope to the stream and then continued along it for quite a while. They saw nothing out of the ordinary. They had lost the trail of the creature quite a ways back, so they were now proceeding on instinct—not their own, but what they thought the creature's instincts would be. Steve reasoned this way: "If I were a dragon lost in the woods, which way would I go?" The truth of the matter was that it was easier to walk downhill than uphill, so that was the way Steve would always find his instinct directing him. After walking for at least a mile, they were becoming fatigued and needed to stop for rest and refreshments. Though Henry carried most of the equipment, Steve made sure that the most essential items had not been left behind—namely the food. They came to a clearing that was almost flat, where the stream spread out into a small pool with tall grasses edging it on three sides. They found a comfortable clump of turf to sit on, and Steve dug into his backpack for a bag of sticky buns he had brought along. Henry, after carrying the lion's share of the load, was considerably more fatigued than Steve, and when he came to the resting spot, he dropped the load at Steve's feet and threw himself on the soft grass.

Henry was just catching his breath and gazing at the sky when he began to ponder their situation. "Steve, you suppose there are real dragons?"

Steve had just taken a big bite of sticky bun, but he didn't let a mouthful of pastry keep him from responding. "Suppose anything is possible. Maybe it's some kind of dinosaur that's come back after millions of years."

Henry sat up. "Like that movie *Drastic Park*?"

"That's *Jurassic Park*, you pea brain, and yes, like that."

Henry was quickly going from a state of curiosity to a place of semianxiety. "So maybe Old Man Stealy was cloning dinosaurs, and the thing we're looking for is one of those things with long sharp teeth and razor-sharp claws that rips humans apart and eats them?"

Mockingly, Steve said, "That's right, Henry. Right now, there's a huge dinosaur lurking in the forest, or maybe even in that tall grass over there, looking for the right time to jump on you and rip your stupid head off your stupid shoulders."

"You think it's crazy, but stranger things have happened. We have no idea what we're dealing with out here." It was then that they heard the rustling in the tall grass. Steve attributed it to the wind, but when Henry noted that there was no wind, they became alarmed. They stood up and turned in the direction the sound came from and listened for more clues. After a few minutes of listening and hearing nothing, Steve came up with a plan that Henry was not too thrilled with. Henry was to walk toward the place they had heard the sounds and poke at the grass using his pole with a loop at the end. If anything appeared, he would put the loop around its neck and subdue it. Steve was to back up Henry with the tranquilizer gun and use it if whatever Henry captured was too much to handle. Henry attempted to disagree with Steve regarding the wisdom of his plan, especially in light of their recent conversation about man-eating dinosaurs, but Steve would hear nothing of it. He reasoned that anything that Henry could not subdue would be well handled by his expert marksmanship with the tranquilizer rifle.

Henry very reluctantly began moving forward, stopping to listen for sounds and carefully poking at the grasses. He tried to get whatever was in there to show itself. Meanwhile, Steve had loaded a cartridge into the tranquilizer gun and had it aimed at the area where Henry was pushing with his pole.

"There's nothing here. Maybe it ran away," Henry called back to Steve, who had placed himself a safe distance from the action.

"Go farther in. I've got you covered." Steve waved the gun, encouraging Henry to be braver than he dared to be. Henry crouched and inched his way farther into the grasses so that only his backside was visible.

"There's something in here, but I can't—" Suddenly Henry let out a blood-curdling scream, and his pole shot straight up in the air, high over the tall grasses, and levitated for a moment above Henry's head. Steve panicked and took a hurried step back, tripping over a stone and falling flat on his back. However, before he fell, his finger flinched on the trigger of the tranquilizer gun, firing a shot that landed squarely in the fatty portion of Henry's buttocks. Henry screamed with pain and gave up all attempts at capturing whatever he had found. He turned around and stumbled back to where Steve was flailing about on his back like a turtle turned upside down. Henry would have run right past Steve, but instead, he tripped on the same stone and fell face-first on top of Steve. Their faces were now pressed against each other.

Henry shouted, "We're going to die!"

Steve shouted back, "What are you talking about?"

"It's going to eat us." Henry had a crazed look in his eyes, and Steve finally muscled him off his chest and onto the grass.

"What did you see?"

By now, the tranquilizer was beginning to take effect, and Henry's words were starting to slur.

"It really is a dragon. It's going to eat us, and we're going to...die." At this, Henry fell unconscious into Steve's arms. Steve had no idea that Henry had been tranquilized and thought that he had somehow been wounded by whatever he had encountered. With adrenaline pumping, Steve slipped into survival mode.

"Stay with me, Henry. I'll get you out of this, buddy. Just hang on." In moments of stress, people say and do strange things. Steve reverted back to all the buddy movies he had seen as a child and began using their old clichés. He hoisted Henry onto his back and somehow found the strength to carry him all the way back to the truck while shouting, "Live, damn you. Live!" Once at the truck, Steve tossed the tranquilized body of Henry into the passenger side of the cab and tore down the road to the local hospital. Because Brandstad's major industry was logging, they had a well-equipped emergency room, so when Steve came to a screeching halt at the front doors, the orderlies were quickly out to his truck with a gurney. They placed the sleeping Henry on it and wheeled him to an examination room while Steve held onto the side of the gurney. He was still shouting encouragements to Henry. "You're going to make it, buddy, and we'll get that dragon together!" Almost delirious, Steve grabbed the lapels of the doctor and told him he had to save his friend because he'd been attacked by a dragon. Once in the examining room, they rolled Henry over and discovered the tranquilizer still firmly implanted in his buttocks.

Outside, Sheriff Joe parked his squad car at the entrance to the emergency room and walked through the front doors. As soon as the nursing staff saw him, they ran up and excitedly told him all they knew of Steve and Henry's adventure, which was often contradictory and mostly unintelligible. Finally, he held up his hand to quiet them and simply said, "Take me to the idiots." They escorted him to the examining room where Henry, still feeling the effects of the tranquilizer, kept muttering, "Run. Run. He's going to kill us all." Except when he said it, it sounded more like, "Rum. Rum. He's mowing to pill us fall." Luckily for Henry, the dosage he had received was about the right amount for an animal of his size, so the only physical effects were a splitting headache and drowsiness, which would last for several hours. The social disgrace of the experience was far greater when word got out. But the humiliation did not decrease the rumors of the dragon, because Henry gave a convincing and vivid description of an enormous creature with huge fangs devouring a carcass, and he added that the creature had turned on him with gargantuan teeth, incredible strength, and lightning speed. Although Steve and Henry were not the most credible of witnesses, the townsfolk were willing to spread the tale, and it grew ever more bizarre with each telling. Sheriff Joe was not convinced and was unwilling to commit law-enforcement resources to finding something that posed no immediate threat to the community. He still believed this was the responsibility of the animal control department, which put solving the mystery back into the hands of Steve and Henry. However, after this debacle, he had little confidence that they would be able to handle whatever was in the forest.

• • •

Thursday was a hard day for Wynona. Beth seemed to be slipping away at an increasing pace, which was demonstrated by the shorter times they were able to spend together before she would drift off to sleep. Although June was doing everything she could not to irritate Wynona, it was a hopeless cause. It was not that what June did caused Wynona agitation; it was more who June was. Wynona had never accepted the fact that she had come from such a conventional woman and therefore couldn't see past the porcelain figurines and the flower arrangements. She longed to have been begotten by an Amelia Earhart—instead, she got Betty Crocker. Of course, this was not June's fault, because if Wynona would have put aside her prejudices, she would have seen that June was fearless in her own homespun way. June had gone on after the death of her husband to successfully run a business and provide college educations for her two daughters. Plus, she did not pursue inferior men in order to gain security. When she found no man who was to her liking, she chose the harder path of being a single mother. These qualities were invisible to Wynona but quite evident to Beth, which was why she had had no problem with coming home and living in the same house with June.

Wynona was caught between two worlds; the new one she was desperately trying to create and the old one that seemed to be chasing her with a dogged determination. She wanted to leave but couldn't, and when it came time for her to go, she knew it would be without her dearest friend. She wanted to hate Brandstad, but some-how, despite all her attempts to make it otherwise, it did feel like home. Most of all, her attraction to Brandon completely baffled her. How could she allow herself to be attracted to someone who had no future? And to top it off, her dreams seemed to be intensifying. She was not a student of psychology, but she knew enough to suspect that the dreams were caused by unresolved issues oozing out in her sleep when she was powerless to contain them. In short, Wynona's life was unraveling. All she really wanted to do was get back to the comfortable, controllable world she had left. With all the talk about a dragon, she was concerned that if she didn't return soon, she might somehow be sucked into the town's mass hallucination.

About midmorning, after the hospice nurse left, Wynona visited Beth in her room, with no intention of telling her about Brandon's ridiculous plan to capture the dragon. What she was hoping for was just a pleasant visit.

Beth didn't waste time deconstructing her plan. "So how was your time with Brandon?"

"Fine," she said, avoiding Beth's eyes.

Unsatisfied with her answer, Beth said, "Fine?"

Desperately trying to avoid any mention of dragons, Wynona said, "Yeah, just fine."

"So what did you do?"

"We cleaned up after the animals in the shelter, and then we went to the Tree Hugger for beers."

"Sounds like fun."

"Kind of."

"Only kind of?"

"It was fun up to a point."

"What point?"

"The point where he got weird on me."

"Weird?"

Wynona felt like a murder suspect on the witness stand with one of those TV lawyers picking apart her alibi. "Yes, weird! He started to talk about dragons again."

"And that's weird?"

Wynona wondered if she had somehow stumbled into a *Twilight Zone* episode because even her normal, level-headed sister was now caught up in the madness. "Yes, he's going out looking for dragons tomorrow morning, and he wants me to go with him."

Beth gave Wynona a wink and a smile. "You should go. It's not every day one can go looking for a dragon."

This exceeded Wynona's tolerance level, even for her sick sister. "If you think I'm going to go tramping through the woods looking for imaginary creatures...Is everybody crazy in this town? There are no such things as dragons!"

"First off, I believe it is just one dragon, and secondly, I believe you have one more favor to do for Brandon. Am I right?"

"How do you know about that?"

Beth reached up and touched a butterfly dangling near her bed. "A little butterfly told me."

"I won't do it. It's too much. It's crazy!"

Beth began to fade again. "So why don't you wear Dad's old army coat? It will keep you warm and maybe bring you good luck."

"No, no, you don't. You can't do that to me again..." But Beth had fallen asleep. Wynona quietly left and stepped into the uncomfortable silence of the adjoining room.

June was still at her shop, and the nurse had posted the stay-away sign on the front door so there would be no visitors. Normally, Wynona would pop open her laptop and busy herself with plans, proposals, and communications, but she was not in the mood for work. Her head was buzzing with all she had experienced the last four days. She still had not gotten an undisturbed night's sleep since she arrived. She decided to take a walk.

It was another bright and flawless day in Brandstad. The wind had picked up slightly from the north, which put a slight chill in the air, but it wasn't anything a light jacket could not handle. She hadn't planned where she was going when she started. She just needed to get out and clear her head. In fact, she really wasn't too aware of her surroundings, because all that was going on inside of her distracted her from noticing anything on the outside. She meandered down to the southern part of town where there were smaller homes, which originally had been built for the itinerant logging workers but had since been renovated into charming two-bedroom cottages. This was also a part of the town where the relatively flat terrain gave way to gentle hills punctuated by several small creeks that wound their way down to the river. Wynona walked aimlessly up one small hill and down another past a small park until she looked up and saw something that took her breath away. She had wandered to the front entrance of a small graveyard adjacent to the oldest church in Brandstad. The church was one of the first structures constructed in town and was typical of those built in the late nineteenth century. It was a quaint, white, wooden building with a steep roof and a bell tower that rung on the hour. Attached to the church was a small annex that had been added in the midfifties but made to perfectly match the architectural design of the church.

Wynona knew why she was here and slowly made her way through the graveyard and up a small hill to a place where a gradual slope looked down upon the town. There she found what she was looking for—the tombstone of Charles W. Swanson. It was a simple gravestone that gave his dates and a small epitaph: Beloved husband, father, and friend to all. It also had a biblical quote: John 15:13, "Greater love has no man then he who gives up his life for his friend." Wynona would often go there as a child and bring wildflowers she had picked or some other object that she thought was beautiful. Sometimes, she would come and sing a little song she had learned or read a poem she had written. On her father's birthday, she would come with Beth and her mother, but those times were not as meaningful to her as when she would come alone. Somehow, she felt especially close to her father when she would just sit and be quiet in this place. In those times, she would try really hard to remember him—the smell of his cologne or the sound of his voice. She would try to recall their times together and reconstruct every part of him she possibly could. But it had been years since she had visited this place, and her heart grieved because she had lost so much of him. It was as if he were fading from her, and all that was left was an emptiness that nothing seemed to fill.

Wynona lay down on the grass next to the grave and began to silently weep. Everything she had tried to keep herself from feeling was now upon her. The sorrow that was always at her door was now let in, and she did not know how to send it away. Then the thought occurred to her that the very place she was lying was probably the place that her sister would be buried in a very short time.

This turned her sorrowful weeping into a sobbing rage. "Why is everyone I love being taken from me?" Wynona felt the hurricane of pent-up emotions sweep over her as she lay there, unable to control any part of herself. She dug her fingers into the grass, as if there was something down there that she desperately needed, and tore open the earth. Finally, after what seemed like an eternity of tears, she rolled over onto her back. She lay still for several minutes and felt the gentle breeze lightly caress her cheeks. Through her water-fogged eyes, she saw the shapes of large tree branches arching over the grave site like protective arms slowly waving in the wind. The leaves on the branches shimmered gently in the breeze as they caught the sunlight and softly reflected it in various shades of green. Then her eyes focused beyond the branches to the incredibly blue sky speckled with wispy white clouds racing across the heavens. They were constantly being transformed by the wind into beautiful shapes. She would pick out one especially lovely cloud and track its movement as it became smaller and smaller until it completely disappeared, only to be replaced by another one that was even lovelier. Wynona breathed in the peace of this place, and her heart began to listen to the rhythm of creation. Without understanding why, she felt peace come over her, and a small bit of her soul awakened.

Meanwhile paranoia was gripping the town, and Mayor Lindquist was feeling the pressure to look like he was addressing the dragon problem. He therefore did what any good politician does—he called a meeting. The city council meeting room was full of talkative and nervous townspeople. Sheriff Joe walked in and took his place at the head table next to Steve and Henry, who were facing the mayor and several council members. Henry was still feeling the effects of the sedative, and his head nodded and bobbed on his shoulders in his attempt to stay awake.

Mayor Lindquist repeatedly struck the gavel on the lectern and shouted in his high, whiny voice, "Order, order, I will have order," but there was no response to his pleas from the buzzing crowd that filled the courthouse. Sheriff Joe was nonchalant as he sat at a table facing the mayor. Then, putting his fingers to his mouth, he let go an ear-splitting whistle, and the room went silent.

"Thank you, Sheriff." The mayor attempted to gather his composure. "We're here to discuss the dangerous situation we find ourselves in and to determine a prudent course of action to remedy it."

Just then a man in overalls, sporting a beard that went below his elbows, stood up and shouted, "I say we go after it right now!" The crowd roared their approval, and the man then sat down glowing as if he had just given the Gettysburg address.

The mayor vainly attempted to quiet the crowd. "Hold on there, Simon. We don't even know what we're going after."

A woman, who could have been the wife of the bearded gentleman, stood up and shouted, "Yeah, we're sure it's dangerous. It killed my little Pookie Bear." Turning to the crowd, she said, "Yeah, that's right. It tore her to shreds till there was nothing left."

Feeling like the situation was getting out of control, the mayor spoke again, his falsetto voice piercing the room. "Now, Helen, we don't know for sure that it was the dragon who got your dog. We do have coyotes."

Another very large lumberjack raised his voice. "So what are you going to do? We've got to do something. That's what we're paying you for!"

A voice from the crowd echoed his argument. "Yeah, people have seen things in the woods that aren't natural. I tell you that we've got a monster on the loose, and I say we call out the National Guard." At the mention of the National Guard, the crowd again erupted in agreement, which drowned out the sound of the impotent gavel being struck by the mayor. The mayor gave a pleading look at Sheriff Joe, and once again, his whistle quieted the crowd.

"Hold on...That's why I called this meeting, and that's why I asked our animal control experts and our sheriff to attend. So if you just let me get on with it, without interruptions, we'll get the answers you're looking for."

Turning to Steve, he said, "Now, Mr. Steven Poup." The mayor pronounced his name like *poop*.

Steve and Henry were sitting behind a table across the aisle from the sheriff and also facing the mayor. Steve immediately shot up his hand. "Uh...Sorry, Mayor Lindquist, that's pronounced *pawup*."

Adjusting his glasses and looking at his notes, the mayor said, "Right, well, you're here to give us your professional opinion since you and your partner are the only ones I know who have actually seen this thing. So tell us, Mr. Poup. What are we dealing with?"

Steve loved it when he was called on to express his opinion, so he put on his most astute air. "Hard to say, Mr. Mayor. What we do know so far is that it's big and dangerous."

Sheriff Joe had been silent so far in the vain hope that the idiot in front of him—the mayor—and the idiots behind—the townspeople—would somehow cancel themselves out, but he could not refrain from challenging the idiot that was sitting across from him. "Dangerous? Just how do you figure that?"

Steve, who had heard the crowd murmur when he said dangerous, felt emboldened to speak. "Well, my partner here almost lost his life in a confrontation with it." The crowd was behind Steve, so he turned to them and spoke with passion. "That's right. I had to rush him to the emergency room in critical condition."

Sheriff Joe waited until the attendees quieted down and then said, "Mayor, the only thing that happened to dumb-ass number two was that dumb-ass number one shot him in the butt with a tranquilizer gun."

As if on cue, Henry, still feeling the effects of the tranquilizer dart, dropped his head on the table. Steve, feeling his rare moment of glory fading, defended himself against the sheriff's criticism. "Yes, it's true. The gun did misfire. But that doesn't explain the gigantic tracks and the dead animal carcasses and the indisputable fact that the thing out there snapped my partner's pole like it was a toothpick." Steve picked up what was left of Henry's pole and placed it before the mayor. "This is exhibit number one."

The mayor examined the pole. "Mr. Poup, this is not a trial." He turned to the other table. "Sheriff, are you saying that there's nothing in those woods?"

A few voices could be heard from the crowd, including a muffled cry, "What about Pookie Bear?"

Attempting to inject some reason into the bizarre event, the sheriff said, "I'm not saying that. I saw the enclosure, and I've examined the tracks. What I am saying is that, so far, there is no hard evidence that it's dangerous. So let's not go off half-cocked and form a posse or anything like that."

Seizing on the word *posse*, the mayor found what he was looking for and shouted, "Excellent idea!"

The sheriff was incredulous. "What?"

Feeling the room sway in his favor, the mayor spoke even more boldly. "We need to form a posse!"

Sheriff Joe felt as if he were in a bad dream. "You're not serious."

"Why not? It's just the thing to address the concerns of Brandstad's residents."

Attempting to stop the momentum that cascaded through the crowd, the sheriff said, "I won't do it. I'm not going to lead a bunch of paranoid fools into the woods to shoot anything that looks like... well, that looks strange. They'll end up shooting each other. No, I'm not that stupid."

Just then Steve saw his moment to recapture the glory. "I am! I mean, I'll do it!"

For all his faults, Mayor Lindquist had good political instincts and saw an opportunity to end the meeting with a solid win. "Good. Then it's settled. Mr. Poup will lead an expedition to find and capture or kill whatever is terrorizing the good people of Brandstad."

Steve, gaining confidence, said, "Meet me Saturday morning at nine o'clock in front of Bill's."

Sheriff Joe knew that some situations, like fires, were not containable, and you just needed to let them burn themselves out. But he couldn't resist one more barb, so he turned to Steve. "You sure that leaves you enough time for breakfast?"

Steve considered the suggestion for a moment and announced to the crowd. "He's right. Make it ten o'clock and bring tracking dogs, and whatever weapons you've got." Everyone in the courtroom was fired up and ready for action, with one fellow shouting, "I've got a shotgun," and another, "I'll bring my hound, Sally. She can find anything!"

Steve, overcome with emotion, climbed onto his chair and scrambled up on the table next to the sleeping Henry. He bellowed, "We're going to get us a dragon!"

• • •

It was early afternoon when Wynona began her walk back from the cemetery to town. For some unknown reason, she decided to stop by June's Flowers and Gifts to visit her mother. She found her working behind the counter wrapping gifts in tissue paper with gold thread. The tinkling bell announced her visit, and her mother looked up and smiled as she stepped into the shop.

June went back to her work. "Out for a little walk?"

Wynona inched her way into the shop. "Yeah, Beth is sleeping, so I thought I could use some fresh air."

"Well, we've got plenty of that around here." June finished a bow. "What do you think?"

Wynona looked down at the small, neatly wrapped box. "Nice. Who is it for?"

"The Stevens's daughter is getting married next weekend, and these are gifts for the reception." June picked up another small box and began to wrap it.

"Dora Stevens is getting married?"

"Yes. To a nice young man she met in college."

Wynona shuffled her feet a bit. She always felt some pressure when it came to the subject of marriage since she was reared in a traditional home that had the unspoken, but very clear, expectation that marriage was the norm, and those who did not marry were somehow departing from it.

"So how many of these do you need to do?"

"See those bags over there?" June pointed to several grocery bags on the floor. "All of those."

The next thing out of Wynona's mouth was completely unexpected by both Wynona and June. "Need any help?"

Before Wynona could retract her unnatural offer, June seized on it. "Yes, that would be lovely, dear."

The rest of the afternoon was spent wrapping boxes and topping them with little bows. If someone had told Wynona that she would be doing this, she would have said she'd sooner slit her wrists, but to her astonishment, she actually found it somewhat enjoyable. She even had a pleasant conversation with her mother on various painless topics. Whether it was because Wynona had grown more tolerant of June or whether June was intentionally avoiding certain subjects, they chatted all afternoon like they were friends. Wynona stayed until closing and walked back to the house with June, and the two of them, along with Beth, enjoyed dinner together. Beth didn't actually eat the food, but June and Wynona brought in trays to her room, and Beth enjoyed what she called her "power shake."

Finally, the day was at an end. Wynona was more tired than she had expected and went to bed early. She had made up a thousand excuses for not going with Brandon on his hunt for the dragon at six in the morning. In fact, she could come up with no good reason why she should go on his harebrained adventure. Still, she had a gnawing feeling that somehow Beth had orchestrated the whole thing and that Wynona was destined to finish the course, wherever it took her.

A wrestling match was taking place within Wynona. On one side was the well-ordered world she had worked so hard to create and pre-serve, and on the other side was an emerging unreasonable desire to go with Brandon. As she slipped off to sleep, she made a decision. If she woke up by five, she would go; if not, she would reject the invi-tation and make excuses to all concerned. Wynona had stacked the odds in her favor. She was not a morning person, and she couldn't remember ever waking up early, unless it was by force. She intention-ally did not set her alarm, because that would, as she put it, "influence the decision." She fell asleep, confident that dragon hunting was not going to be a part of her future, and whatever fate had planned for her, it would not be in the woods at six the next morning. She was wrong.

14
Into the Woods

WYNONA'S CAR PULLED up in front of Old Man's Stealy's house just as the first rays of the sun touched the tops of the trees. Brandon's Jeep was already there, but there was no sign of him. There was a nip in the air as Wynona stepped out of her car and zipped up the oversized military fatigue jacket she was wearing, which had belonged to her father. It had his name bar above the pocket and his sergeant stripes on the sleeves. She looked around and was beginning to have the rather pleasant feeling that he had left without her when a voice came from behind the house.

"Swanson, that you?" She shouted back, "Yeah, it's me," and then under her breath added, "Stupid, crazy, clueless me."

Brandon emerged from around the corner of the house dressed in his wizard outfit. "You surprised me. I honestly didn't think you'd come."

"Yeah, well, never underestimate my idiocy or Beth's stubbornness. So what are we going to do, and do you need to be dressed like that?"

Brandon reached into his Jeep, pulled out his knapsack, and slung it over his back. "This is what I dress like when I am on a quest."

"Is that what we are on, a quest?"

"Don't get your khakis in a bunch, sergeant. We are all looking for something. Think of a quest as an especially committed and condensed search."

"I'm not looking for anything but a good night's sleep, which I did not get, so the sooner we get this thing done the sooner I can go home and get what I'm looking for."

Brandon came close to Wynona, who was trying in vain to avoid looking at him. "Wynona, you don't really know what you're looking for, and that's the saddest part."

"Well, it certainly isn't a dragon. That much I know!" But Brandon wasn't listening. He had already started into the forest. Wynona, left standing by the Jeep, heaved a deep sigh and followed him into the woods.

The forest was cool and wet from the morning dew. They followed the same path that Steve and Henry had taken the day before, which led them down to the small stream. Along the trail, Brandon would periodically stop and examine a flower or a bush and occasionally clip off a few leaves with his knife or collect berries and put them in a leather pouch that hung on his belt. Wynona rolled her eyes and thought to herself that he was the poster child for those who stop and smell the roses. They continued to walk beside the stream until they came to the place where Steve and Henry had their encounter. Brandon pushed aside the tall grass to reveal a deer carcass that had been almost entirely devoured. All that was left were a few scattered bones and the skull. Brandon walked carefully around the scene looking for clues. He saw a remnant of Henry's broken pole. He also noticed the same tracks heading off downstream, the same type that were seen at Old Man Stealy's place.

Wynona had been following a short distance behind Brandon. The first thing she noticed was a package of discarded sticky buns. She stepped forward to where Brandon was crouching, and she saw the carcass and the pole. She felt, for the first time, that there might just be something behind all the paranoia.

"What happened here? Did your dragon kill this animal?"

"No, this deer was taken down by a mountain lion. You can see the tracks. But there was something else here that finished off the carcass. You can see its marks here and there, and then it moved off in that direction." Brandon pointed down the path.

"So what now?" Wynona cringed in anticipation of the answer.

"Now we go and find it."

"Find what?"

"You don't want to know."

"You're right."

They hiked in the downward direction of the stream. But this time, Wynona noticed that Brandon was more cautious and took his time at places where the foliage obscured the path. This made Wynona even more anxious, and she really didn't know if she should follow close to him or hang back just in case something horrible popped out. She also noticed again that he walked with a confidence she didn't remember him having when they were dating. In fact, there was an air of authority in his manner that appealed to her. He seemed like a man on a mission, and his confidence came from a commitment to it. She was beginning to admire him now that she realized he was completely different. She thought to herself that he could be quite successful in business if he could somehow harness his energy for something productive rather than searching for dragons.

They walked on for several miles until midday. Wynona realized she was beginning to get hungry and she hadn't thought to bring any food. Maybe Wynona didn't "do breakfast," but that didn't mean she didn't eat. She usually subsisted on a hearty lunch and a small dinner. But at this point, she was doubting the hearty lunch, and she didn't even want to think about dinner.

Eventually, they came to a place where the stream widened out into a pond. There, Brandon stopped and put down his pack. Wynona came up from behind and threw herself on the ground next to the pond. "Hey, Mr. Wizard, what do you plan to conjure up for lunch?"

"Are you hungry?" Brandon reached into his pack and began to pull out small containers.

"Famished." She rolled over and propped herself up on her elbows. "So hungry I could eat...a dragon."

"Well, that's not on the menu, but I hope you'll like what I prepare." He placed the small containers around him, and then pulled out the various leaves, roots, and berries he had collected along the trail.

Wynona looked at the assortment of containers and all the foliage. "Let me guess—organic?"

"Far better than organic. This is straight from the woods." He proceeded to wash some of the vegetation in the stream and cut it up in bite-size pieces. He placed it in a large wooden bowl that he had pulled from his pack. Then he opened the small containers, sprinkled or poured the contents over the greens in the bowl, and began to toss what looked more and more like the ultimate garden salad. Brandon plucked out of his bag a couple of wooden forks, handed one to Wynona, and smiled. "Bon appétit."

"You mean you've been collecting our lunch while we've been walking? How do you know this stuff is safe?" As hungry as Wynona was, she was not ready to dig into what she considered to be weeds.

Brandon stuck his fork into the middle of his creation and put a large helping of salad into his mouth. Then he began to point to each individual plant in the bowl. "This is *Agoseris*, commonly called dandelion, and it has been eaten for millennia. And this is an arrowhead leaf, very tasty and nutritious. This little flower is a marsh marigold and quite edible. I have also added knotweed seeds and berries from the false Solomon's seal. This forest can feed us, if we just know what to eat."

Wynona was still hesitant to trust her stomach to Brandon. "And you know what to eat because..."

"Let's just say the forest and I have become friends, and she's shared her secrets with me."

"The forest talks to you?"

"OK, I took a course in woodcraft from the community college, but it's more an art than a science to make a feast like this one."

Wynona continued to be skeptical, but her stomach was beginning to growl loudly. She watched Brandon take one bite after another without any apparent ill effects, so she took her fork and tentatively speared a few pieces of what appeared to be spinach—though she knew it was not—and slowly put them in her mouth. She really didn't know what to expect, but what she experienced was a tangy, sweet taste unlike anything she had ever eaten. It was not unpleasant, just completely unfamiliar and therefore not easily described. Brandon watched her for some indication as to how she liked his recipe, but Wynona was too proud to let on that she might have been too hasty in rejecting his lunch.

Brandon looked at Wynona with a combination of amusement and sincere affection. What did he see in her? Yes, she was a beautiful woman, and there was definitely chemistry between them, but for Brandon, it went well beyond the physical attraction. Brandon was a true lover and restorer. He sought out those who were lost, abandoned, and wounded and went beyond sympathy—he sought their salvation, not in a religious sense but in a very practical one. He worked in the animal shelter because he saw the animals he cared for as being in need of someone to help save them from neglect and abuse, and when he looked at Wynona, he saw the same thing. To Brandon, Wynona was just as lost and broken as a wild animal that had been damaged and left by the road to die. When an injured creature came into the shelter, it was often scared and in pain and more likely to bite the helper than to gladly receive care. In Brandon's eyes, Wynona's sarcastic jabs at him were no different than that. He more than tolerated her because he understood her and was not offended when she struck out at him in her pain. This attitude confused and befuddled Wynona, who had crafted a world in which she hid her weaknesses behind a hard shell of invulnerability. She could only attribute his failure to respond negatively to her criticisms as his ignorance and naiveté. But being in the woods with him and seeing how he navigated this foreign world with such confidence had created a conflict of emotions within her. How could someone who seemed so sure of himself be so committed to something that was so obviously unreal?

They finished their lunch, and Brandon cleaned the utensils in the stream and packed them back in his bag. It was now early afternoon, and they were still no closer to finding whatever they were looking for, so she asked the obvious question.

"Don't you think it's time we turned around and headed back to town?"

"That's not what we do when we're on a quest."

"Oh, sorry, Mr. Wizard. So what do people do when they are on a quest in the middle of nowhere and they can't find what they're after?"

"First, we are not in the middle of nowhere, and second, we are very close to finding what we are looking for." Brandon picked up his pack and began heading downstream on the small path. Wynona picked herself up off the ground and looked around. Her options were simple: She could turn back and head to her car, which seemed a pretty daunting task since seeing the carcass had made her fairly anxious about what she would encounter on the return trip. Or, she could continue to follow her guide, who seemed confident of success. She stood frozen for a moment in indecision as Brandon moved on down the trail. It became clear that option two was less unpleasant than option one, at least at the moment. "Hey, wait up," she shouted to her disappearing guide.

When she caught up with Brandon, he turned around. "Had a moment of indecision, huh?"

"Shut up. I figure I'm safer with you because whatever is out here might eat you before it comes after me."

"Thanks for your concern." Brandon turned around and resumed his careful and deliberate tracking of the unknown creature.

"So are you ever going to let me know what you think we're going to find out here?"

"I'd rather not fill your mind with what I think until I'm sure. I don't want to alarm you needlessly."

"Oh, that's comforting."

They walked on for about another hour. Every once in a while, Brandon would stop and carefully explore a patch of tall grass or a crevice between rocks. He would often ask Wynona to stand at a safe distance when he came across a place that caused him concern. This went on until they came to another of the many areas where the stream broadened out into a shallow pool. There, he stopped and slowly inspected the ground as he walked around the pond to a large outcropping of rocks on the other side, where a small waterfall fed into the stream. He found a small cave that was just large enough for several people to fit into and he paused in front of it.

Brandon then waved at Wynona, who was finding it amusing to splash in the shallow pool. She also attempted to skip rocks on the placid surface. "Wynona, would you please stand back while I check this out?" He gently pushed back some tall grass that partly obscured the opening of the small cave.

Wynona, frustrated with his seemingly needless caution, came up behind him.

"What the hell, Brandon? You've been looking all day for something that I'm pretty sure doesn't exist, so let's just turn around, and you can go on your quest tomorrow without me."

Brandon was so fixed upon his investigation of the cave that he didn't see her come up close behind him as he pushed back the grass. It was then that they saw it, but it was too late. Out of the cave came the largest, scariest creature Wynona had ever seen. It was at least six feet long and had an enormous snout and a set of hideous teeth.

It came rushing out toward them, and Brandon, in one swift move, swept up Wynona and placed her on a ledge just above the cave. He quickly scrambled up behind her. The creature launched itself forward with amazing speed, and they watched as it belly-flopped into the pond and then slowly turned around to face them. They stared in astonishment at its large snout and enormous flared nostrils as it sniffed the air like it was attempting to locate its next meal.

Wynona let out a muffled scream: "Dragon!" She had the overwhelming impulse to run, but there was no place to go. The ledge they were sitting on was just above the opening of the cave and was cut out of a sheer rock face at least thirty feet high. The only way down was by the way they had gotten up, and that would be directly in the path of the creature.

If Brandon was anxious, he didn't show it. He sat for several minutes examining the beast. "Wynona, I want you to meet the terror of Brandstad." Wynona would have said something witty or sarcastic at this moment, but all she could do was clutch Brandon's arm in horror. The creature seemed in no hurry to do anything. It thrashed about in the water and then waddled uncomfortably close to where the two were sitting. Finally, Wynona found her voice and was able to barely squeak out, "What is it?"

"It's a dragon."

"Really?"

Brandon looked on the creature with a steady gaze and spoke softly and slowly. "It's a Komodo dragon, the largest reptile on earth. It's very rare." Wynona's fears were not diminished by Brandon's matter-of-fact attitude, especially since she felt that knowing what it was would not stop it from making her its next victim.

"Oh, fine. One should always know the proper name of the thing that's going to eat her."

"They very rarely attack humans, so I don't think we're in too much danger." Wynona slowly grasped the full size of the creature as her eyes fixated on its large row of ragged teeth and what appeared to be green moss hanging from its mouth.

"OK, you've found your dragon. Now let's get the hell out of here."

"That's not why I came out here. I intend to save it."

"Save it! Are you crazy? That dragon's looking at us like we're its next meal."

"Don't think so. It had a pretty full meal only a day ago. They have a slow metabolism and only need to eat about twelve times a year."

"So why is it looking at us like that?"

Brandon shifted on the rock, and the Komodo dragon began to follow his movements. "It's probably just curious."

"OK, so let's say it's not looking to eat us. Why don't we just leave it alone and live and let live?"

"Because if we leave it out here, it will die. Its natural environment is the tropics. It will never survive our winter."

"Better him than us."

Brandon then reached into his pack and took out a long hemp rope. Wynona looked at him with astonishment. "No, you're not going to do what I think you're going to do." Brandon made a noose with one end of the rope and slowly climbed down from the rock. "Brandon, no. Please don't do that. I do not want to be left alone in this godforsaken place."

Brandon turned to Wynona. "Don't you understand? Old Man Stealy kept this Komodo dragon for nobody knows how long, fed it carrion, and kept it at a temperature that allowed it to survive. I've got to get it someplace where it won't die."

"So you intend to put a leash on it and take it back. Is that right?"

"It's the only way." Brandon carefully climbed down the rock face and began to approach the creature.

"Here's another idea. Why don't we just go back to town, tell them where it is, and let the experts come and take it to wherever it needs to go?"

At that point, Brandon was slowing approaching the Komodo dragon, which stood in the shallow pond, rocking its head back and forth. "Because those guys would sooner kill it than capture it. They see it just like you do—as dangerous—because of their ignorance."

Wynona was out of options. All she could do was sit and watch the last quest of a fool, but what happened next astonished her. Instead of fighting the noose, the creature seemed to welcome Brandon and was as docile as a well-trained hound. Brandon gently slipped the rope about the its thick head and stood looking up at the cowering Wynona with a combination of wonderment and joy. Then, he announced, "You can come down now."

"OK, cowboy, you've lassoed the creature, but how do you think you're going to get him all the way back to the Jeep?"

Before he could answer, there was a sudden clap of thunder. Because their interest had been so focused upon the creature, they had not noticed the change in the weather. Thunderstorms came up very quickly in the mountains, and they could strike with great intensity.

Wynona cried, "Oh, great. What else could happen? God, why do you hate me?" Brandon was unfazed by the approaching storm and quickly looked about for shelter.

"Let's go back into the cave until it blows over."

"What do you mean? I'm not going in there with that...thing!" But Brandon was already leading the dragon into the small cave, which turned out to be surprisingly spacious.

"Suit yourself, but Pete and I are going to get out of the rain."

"Pete? You've named that thing Pete?"

"Yeah, it was one of my favorite movies when I was a kid, and I think it fits." He looked down at the dragon. "Right, Pete?" As if on cue, the dragon rocked his head in what appeared to be a nod. "See. He likes it." Large drops of rain began to splatter on the rock around Wynona as a strong wind picked up from the north. Wynona once again had a difficult choice: sit in the open during an intense thunderstorm or join Brandon and his new friend, Pete, in the shelter of the cave. She climbed down off the rock, approached the opening of the cave, peered in, and saw that Brandon and Pete had already found a dry, semicomfortable spot in the back of the cave. She muttered something inaudible and hesitated in front of the cave. A bolt of lightning struck nearby and a huge clap of thunder shook the earth, which caused her to take an involuntary leap into the cave. Once there, Brandon, Pete, and Wynona sat for what seemed to her like hours while the storm roared outside. Wynona periodically peered outside and saw the small gentle stream slowly grow faster and larger. She wondered if their end might come with being swept away by a flood. She could not tell how much time had passed, but it was clear that it would soon be nightfall, and Wynona was preparing for the worst night of her life. She pulled her father's coat close about her and thought, *Some luck this jacket is*. Finally, she said what she thought had to be said: "So it's going to be dark soon. Don't suppose you thought to bring a flashlight?"

"No flashlight."

"No flashlight? What kind of idiot goes into the forest without a flashlight?"

"The kind of idiot who doesn't bring cell phones, tents, or camp stoves. We live in and off the forest."

"Oh, I forgot. Well, since you're a wizard, why don't you just conjure up one. Or at least start a fire so we don't have to sit here all night in the dark."

"I could do that, but I don't think Pete would be too happy about it. He's already pretty nervous with all the lightning."

"By all means, let's think of the big lizard first. We wouldn't want to frighten him."

"Wynona, I know this is not what you expected, and I'm sorry about the potential of an uncomfortable evening, but sometimes life is unexpected. Can't we make the best of it and call it an adventure rather than a trial?" Wynona stared hard at Brandon in the ever-increasing gloom and thought to herself that he was either the most well-adjusted person she had ever known or the most clueless. Right then, she was leaning heavily toward clueless.

After what seemed like an eternity, the storm abated until only distant flashes of lightning pierced the opening of the cave. Wynona sat facing outward because she couldn't bear looking at Pete, but also partly because she was searching for the very first opportunity to flee the uncomfortable living arrangement. As she peered out into the darkness, she thought she saw something silhouetted by the flashes of distant lightning. She couldn't tell what it was, but it resembled the shape of a man. *This is just too much. Now I'm having hallucinations. Maybe it was something Brandon picked this afternoon for lunch*, she thought to herself.

Then there was another distant flash, and she saw, without a doubt, the outline of a man standing at the mouth of the cave. Once again, fear struck her speechless.

15
The Abbey

FROM THE SHADOWY figure came an intense beam of light that struck Wynona in the face. The beam then turned to illuminate both Brandon and Pete.

"Hello, in the cave. Are you two OK?"

Wynona was still striving to calm her racing heart and retrieve her voice. All she could do was nod her head. From behind her came Brandon's voice. "We're good in here. We're just waiting for the storm to pass." Wynona had just calmed herself enough to speak when she heard Brandon's nonchalant appraisal of their situation. She leaped to her feet and rushed out of the cave, nearly knocking the man off his feet.

"We are not good. We are far from good. I am stuck out in the woods with someone who didn't even have the sense to bring a flashlight and who is now best friends with the largest, ugliest lizard I have ever seen."

Once Wynona stepped away from the cave, she was able to get a look at her rescuer. She noticed that he was wearing a robe. At this point, there was absolutely no filter between Wynona's thoughts and her words, and she addressed the man standing before her.

"Oh, great, another wizard. Is this place full of wizards?"

The man chuckled and then turned his light on the mouth of the cave where Brandon and Pete were just emerging.

"So you found him." And he reached down and gently patted Pete's nose.

Wynona looked at the affectionate way the man treated Pete. "You two know each other?"

"Well, sort of. We're neighbors. Maybe I should explain. I'm Brother John, and I live in the monastery on the other side of the hill. Bernie was my friend, and I would often come by and visit him and his animals. This Komodo dragon was his favorite. When I heard Bernie died and that our friend here had escaped, I set out to look for him. I knew he wasn't going to survive in the forest alone. I got caught in the rainstorm like you and was heading for the cave when I found you."

Brandon looked down at the stooping man. "I call him Pete."

"Pete. I like that." Brother John stood up and looked at the two. "So who does Pete owe his rescue to?"

"I'm Brandon, and this is Wynona."

"Very happy to meet you both." He took a look at Brandon's robe. "A LARPer, right?"

"Right! You know about LARPs?"

Brother John chuckled again. "We occasionally meet them in the forest, and we admire one another's robes. So how would you two like to come have dinner and spend the night at the monastery?"

Brandon hesitated. "We really need to be getting Pete back to the shelter—"

Wynona interrupted. "We're happy to take you up on your offer, especially since you are the only one who brought a flashlight and seems to know where he's going. I assume you have a telephone so I can tell my mother that I haven't been kidnapped."

Brother John smiled. "Of course. We even have indoor plumbing."

"OK, I'm in too." Brandon knew when he was outnumbered.

"Good. Then follow me, and we should be there within the hour."

The four of them followed the trail downstream to a place where it split into two paths. One path continued to follow the stream, and the other headed upward, took a couple of switchback turns, and then crested upon a small mesa. The storm clouds had moved off to reveal a quarter moon and a brilliant canopy of stars. Brother John turned off his flashlight, lifted his head to the sky, and whispered, "The heavens declare the glory of God."

Wynona and Brandon followed Brother John's example and also looked up. They were shocked by the intensity of the light produced by the night sky. Wynona especially was struck by its beauty. She had spent so much time in the city where the stars were obscured by artificial light that she had forgotten what a truly unencumbered night sky looked like. Brandon, on the other hand, often looked up and drank in the night sky, but this night was more intense than any he could remember.

They'd stood speechless for several moments when Brother John broke the silence. "I come up here often when I need an attitude adjustment. I find that it puts all things into perspective." Brother John turned his flashlight back on and continued on the trail. "We're almost there."

After a short distance, Brandon spoke. "I have lived here all my life, and I never knew there was a monastery nearby."

"That's not surprising. We like to fly under the radar. It helps us fulfill our mission."

"And what mission is that?" Wynona was realizing that she knew nothing about Brother John, his monastery, or his mission, and she was concerned that she might have jumped at his invitation too quickly.

"We are a place of healing, and we find solitude a key ingredient."

Wynona probed further. "So what are you, some kind of convalescent hospital?"

"You might say that. However, we focus on the healing of both body and spirit."

Perfect, Wynona thought, *we're going to spend the night in a mental hospital. Maybe it will do Brandon some good.*

Brandon was listening intently to Brother John and was eager to learn more. "Sounds fascinating," he said. They turned a corner at the bottom of the hill and walked through a small grove of trees until they came upon a large, stately home that could have easily been transported from an English countryside. It was constructed of stone and had a large circular driveway in front. Like the homes in town, its slate roof was pitched steeply to deal with the heavy winter snows, and tower-like structures formed the four corners of the large building. In the center was an enormous, ornate wooden door that was wide enough for a small car to drive through.

"Here it is, your home for the night." Brother John walked up to the front doors and was about to invite his guests in when he stopped. "Oh my, I almost forgot. We've got to find a place for Pete. I don't think he would much care to be in the house, and frankly, some of our guests might not understand him as we do."

Wynona thought to herself, *Right. Those would be the normal ones.* They took a path that led around the house and came to a beautiful English garden artistically lit with accent lights that allowed it to be appreciated even in the dark. At the end of the garden was a large gate through which they came upon a tool shed. Brother John opened the door and turned on the light. "Yes, I think this will do nicely. Only you must remind me to tell Pedro, our gardener, that Pete is in here. I would hate to surprise him in the morning." Brandon led a very obedient Pete into the shed, and Brother John turned off the light and closed the door. "Do you suppose he will need anything to eat tonight?"

Brandon replied, "No, he had a pretty large meal yesterday, and according to all my research, they don't eat too frequently."

"Really? Sounds like you've done your homework on Komodo dragons," Brother John said with admiration.

"I heard about the sightings and examined the tracks and figured it was either a Komodo dragon or a crocodile."

"Crocodile? You thought we were chasing a crocodile? Those things kill people!" Wynona was again astounded by Brandon's recklessness.

"Well, yes, but not if you're careful and don't take chances."

"This whole stupid quest has been one big chance. I just want it to be over."

Brother John interjected, "I think everyone will feel a lot better with a little warm food and maybe a glass of our own vintage caber- net. What do you say we go into the abbey and have dinner?" Brandon and Wynona just nodded and followed Brother John.

They walked back through the garden, and this time, Wynona took a bit more notice of where she was. The garden was laid out like a traditional English walled garden with vine-covered partitions punctuated by openings that led into alcoves of bubbling fountains. These were surrounded by beds of roses and other fragrant flowers. Wynona loved gardens, and she would have explored this one if she had not been so hungry, but what she glimpsed made her want to come back in the morning and see it in the sunlight. Brother John led them across a stone terrace to a set of large windowed doors that opened to an expansive wood-paneled room dotted by round tables and overstuffed leather chairs. She thought to herself that this was not what she expected a monastery to look like—not that she had thought too much about a monk's habitat, but somehow, she expected it to be more Spartan and cold. In the corner was a large stone fireplace where a fire glowed, lending the room a comfort- able and cozy feeling. Brother John invited them to sit and relax, but before she got comfortable, Wynona asked to be shown to the phone so she could check in with June on Beth's condition. June assured her that Beth was sleeping comfortably and that she would not miss her for one evening. June also secretly thought that an evening away would be good for Wynona, and when she heard that she was staying in a monastery for the evening, she couldn't help but think this might be an answer to her prayers. Wynona was reluctant to be away from Beth, but June assured her that she would call if there was any sudden change in Beth's condition. With her fears reduced, Wynona agreed to stay the night at the abbey. Besides, she was hungry and tired, and the monastery was turning out to be far more comfortable than she had expected.

When Wynona returned, Brother John brought out a bottle of wine and glasses, uncorked the bottle, and poured the richest and most flavorful red wine Wynona had ever tasted. He then whispered to another monk who was also dressed in a simple robe but with the addition of an apron, and he went off toward what Wynona guessed was the kitchen.

Wynona began to feel a bit more relaxed and ventured to ask questions. "Excuse me for my ignorance, but this is not what I expected a monastery to look like."

Brother John took a sip of wine and smiled. "What did you expect?"

"Well, you know, more austere surroundings, more..."

Sensing that Wynona was searching for a word that would not offend him, Brother John finished her sentence. "Religiously uptight?"

Feeling a bit ungrateful for questioning her host, she said, "Yes, I guess you could say that."

Brother John laughed a warm and free laugh. "There are all kinds of monks and all kinds of monasteries, some plain and some not so plain. Each has its purpose. This is a house of healing, so we keep it in a way that brings beauty and joy to those who come here."

Brandon was more interested in drinking in the beauty of his surroundings and enjoying the excellent wine, but he also had a question. "Brother John, you said that this is a place of healing. Who comes here to be healed? Is this a hospital?"

"There are all kinds of wounds and all kinds of places to be healed. This is a place for those who are wounded in spirit, a place of prayer and meditation. We create an environment of quiet beauty where God can restore those who are tired, weary, and discouraged."

Brother John's words resonated with Brandon, but for Wynona, they created a slight uneasiness. She resisted quiet contemplation because it only made her more aware of the pain she was trying hard to suppress. She somehow sensed that if she spent too much time in a place like this, it would only deepen the wounds in her life, not heal them. After a short while, the other monk brought out a tray full of freshly baked bread, homemade soup, perfectly prepared vegetables, and chicken grilled to perfection. It was indeed a meal that could satisfy any hunger. The three enjoyed the meal and conversed about topics that would not make Wynona uncomfortable. Finally, after they had eaten all they wanted, Brother John guided them to their rooms and bid them a good night's sleep. He also gave them an invitation.

"Breakfast is at seven, but if you would like to join us for morning prayers at six, you are more than welcome." Wynona did not want to offend her host, so she said that she would consider his offer if she rose early. Brandon, on the other hand, seemed honestly enthusiastic and asked where to find the morning prayers.

Brother John chuckled and said, "Just follow the music. All our prayer services are filled with music." Before Brother John left them, he turned to Wynona, put his hand upon her shoulder, and spoke in a compassionate voice. "Wynona, there are no accidents. I was led to discover you and Brandon in the woods tonight, and I welcome you to find whatever healing that this place offers you." His words penetrated to her heart, and all she could do was turn away and say thank you. She then disappeared into her room before anyone could see the tears forming in her eyes. Once in her room, she told herself she was emotional because of all that had happened that day, and maybe she had drunk too much wine. But she knew differently. She was one of those wounded souls that Brother John spoke of, and she felt the weight of the fear and frustration in her life stirring from deep within her like a volcano about to erupt. But she would not let that happen—she was in control, and she would not let her hopeless emotions take her where she did not want to go.

Wynona's room was not fancy, but again, it was very comfortable. It had a soft bed and a large window opening to a balcony that looked out upon the spacious garden. Clean towels and a beautiful white cotton nightgown and robe were laid out upon the bed. A private bathroom adjacent to her room had everything she could need to take a leisurely hot bath. She thought, *These people really know hospitality. They should go into the hotel business.* She treated herself to a long, luxurious soak and then put on the nightgown, which was fragranced with lilac. That was when she heard the music. It seemed to come from beneath her window, and she quickly put on her robe and stepped out onto the small balcony. Below her, in the garden, was a string quartet made up of monks playing in the garden. The music was ethereal and seemed to float upon the warm summer breeze to her room. She stood listening, gazing upon the luminous garden, transfixed as if she were in a dream. She lifted her head once again to see the brilliant night sky. Her mind went back to a time when she was a little girl looking out her window and wondering if one of those points of light was where her father was, waiting for her. She would have been content to stay forever in such a place where there were no deadlines, no competition, and no endless series of disappointments. But her reverie was interrupted.

"Beautiful, isn't it?"

Wynona gasped. It seemed like the voice was coming from directly behind her. Then it spoke again.

"The music, I mean."

Wynona turned to her right and noticed that there on the balcony adjacent to hers, Brandon was leaning on his own railing not more than ten feet from her.

"It's OK, if you're into that sort of thing."

"Are you into that sort of thing, Wynona?"

Wynona could not help but soften. After all, wasn't it every woman's dream to be serenaded while standing upon a balcony above a beautiful garden? "Yes, I must admit I am."

"You know, when I saw you standing there in the starlight listening to the music, I couldn't make my mind up what was more beautiful."

"More beautiful?"

"The stars, the music, or you, but I think I have come to a decision."

"You have?"

"It's you."

Wynona rarely blushed, but she could feel a flush come into her cheeks. She turned away to avoid Brandon's gaze. Attempting to change the subject, she said, "So what happens tomorrow?"

"Tomorrow? I guess we take Pete back to Brandstad, and I begin looking for his new home."

The blush had passed, and Wynona felt it was safe to turn back toward Brandon. "Then what?"

"What do you mean?"

"I mean, what are you doing here, Brandon? Why are you wasting your life in this backward little town? You could do so much more." Wynona's tone was not angry or even accusatory; she genuinely believed what she was saying, and her words came out in a pleading tone. "Don't you see that if you hang out with a bunch of losers, you'll never get anywhere?"

"And just where do you think I should go, Wynona? Do you think I should go to the city like you and get a big job like you and make money like you?"

"Why not?"

"Because I don't want to become miserable like you."

"Fine! Hang out with your LARP friends and dress up like storybook characters and run around the woods and see where it gets you."

"Wynona, being a LARPer is not who I am, but it helps me to open myself to wonders that most of us are too busy to see. Being here with the stars filling the sky and the music filling the night air, don't you feel it? Don't you sense that there's something wonderful that we just can't quite touch except through a fleeting glimpse here or an unexpected thought there?"

Wynona looked at Brandon as he spoke, but she was not hearing his words; she was looking at his eyes, and she saw an excitement that she never knew existed. In the world she lived in, eyes were cold and gray; they were filled with hunger for money, power, or pleasure, but not with wonder. And for a moment, she remembered a day in the woods with her father and his look of total joy when they found an especially beautiful butterfly. There was magic in her father's eyes, and she saw the same magic in the eyes of Brandon. Suddenly, an overwhelming sense of sadness came upon her as she felt the poverty of her own life in comparison to the riches that Brandon was experiencing. What she said next did not come from her head but from deep within her heart, where she had no power to control.

"That part of me is dead. It died with my father, and if that wasn't enough to kill it, then it's dying with Beth right now! So don't tell me life is wonderful. Don't lie to me—I can't stand to be lied to!" Wynona's voice cracked with emotion, and she felt the tears welling up in her eyes. She ran into her room, threw herself on her bed, and buried her face in her pillow so no one would hear her violent sobs.

Brandon stood for a while on his balcony looking out at the evening. The musicians had finished, and all that could be heard was the sound of crickets and a distant owl making its solitary presence known. He thought about Wynona and why she was in so much pain. Beth's sickness had caused everyone grief, and he was already preparing himself for the time of mourning when she died. But Wynona's pain was there before Beth's illness, and it was apparent that it would remain long after her passing. Brandon felt powerless to reach out to Wynona. He didn't know what to say, and whatever he did say seemed to only make matters worse. He also didn't know how to give her what she needed most—hope. She seemed to be trapped in a deep pit of pain that only became more excruciating when anyone tried to help her escape. He thought it would take a miracle, some sort of divine intervention, to save Wynona from her self-imposed prison, and he did not know what that miracle might be. Then he thought if there ever was a place for miracles to happen, just maybe a monastery would be the place. After all, it really seemed miraculous that they'd found Pete and that the three of them had ended up with Brother John in this place. So maybe the miracle was coming.

Brandon turned in for the night and had a much more restful sleep than Wynona did. She was still haunted by images of the last night she'd seen her father and her desperate attempt to save him.

16
Why Are You Weeping?

WYNONA AWOKE TO the sound of chanting men. For a brief moment of disorientation, she didn't remember where she was and thought she had left the radio on. But then she opened her eyes and remembered. Sunlight was flooding in through the balcony windows, and a warm breeze gently caused the sheer curtains to billow and hang loose. She remembered Brother John's invitation to attend morning prayers, and for no apparent reason, she was favorably inclined to accept it. She was a bit mystified by her willingness to do something that she normally would have avoided at all costs. But nothing seemed normal since coming back to Brandstad, so she decided her interest in monks praying shouldn't be any different.

She dressed quickly and stepped out into the corridor, where she listened for the music to guide her to the chapel. The hallway was as well appointed as the rest of the building. Works of art depicting various biblical scenes adorned the walls and beautiful porcelain statues were strategically placed on antique wooden tables. She stopped to look at the artwork, thinking that her mother would appreciate the statues. This thought also surprised her. Wynona listened intently for the music and followed it down the hallway to a set of winding stairs and then through another large hall that ended in a pair of ornate wooden doors. She carefully opened the doors to reveal an intimate chapel bathed in multicolored lights. Wynona cautiously stepped into the room and immediately placed herself in the back pew so that, if it became necessary, she could make a hasty escape. She looked up. The chapel was as tall as it was long, and on each side arose an uninterrupted wall of stained glass, the source of the brilliant light. Her eyes could barely take in the intensity of the images as the sun made them sparkle and shine. She was drawn to an especially beautiful mosaic in the center of the chapel, just above the altar. The position of the sun was such that this pane was the brightest of them all, and it was, without a doubt, the most colorful. Her eyes slowly adjusted to the sunlight pouring through this window, and when they did, she gasped. The light was in the shape of a magnificent butterfly with its wings outstretched. Wynona did not believe in signs, but if she did, this would have been one. Her attention then turned to the music.

Brandon had risen earlier and checked on Pete, and when he heard the music, he too followed it until he came to the chapel. But instead of timidly slipping into a back row, he boldly made his way to the front and took a seat among the brothers who were filling the first few rows of the chapel. To Brandon, this was all an adventure to be savored, so when the brothers began to sing, he joined in with a full voice, even though he was unfamiliar with the melody and the words. Brandon possessed a heart that was open and soft to the mysteries of life; he was blessed with the quality of humility, which allowed him to admit his ignorance and be open to instruction from those who were farther down the road of life. Brandon saw in Brother John just such a person, and he had committed in his heart to make this amazing man a personal mentor. When Brother John stepped up to the podium, Brandon was transfixed. Brother John played an acoustic guitar and began singing in his deep baritone voice.

> Blessed be the God who created us.
> Blessed be the God who sustains.
> Blessed be the God who fills the earth

And showers blessings like gentle rain.
Blessed be the one who comes to him
With broken wings in pain.
Blessed is the one who sits in silence
And comes to life again.

The rest of the brothers joined in on the chorus and sang:

Alleluia, we are loved.
Alleluia, to the King.
Alleluia, we are made new.
Alleluia, he has given us wings.

The service went on for a while longer with a well-choreographed blending of music, prayers, and recitations, which all centered upon the healing power of God, but for Wynona, the most meaningful aspect of the service was the stained-glass window of the butterfly. The more she stared at it the more lifelike it became. At one point in the service, whether it was caused by an optical illusion or she had somehow been put into a trancelike state, the stained-glass butterfly left its two-dimensional world and took flight over the congregation, where it soared above their heads. At this point, she was completely unaware of whatever else was taking place in the service.

"Wynona, are you hungry for breakfast?" Wynona broke her gaze at the window and turned to see a smiling Brother John standing next to her.

Still dazed by her vision, she asked, "Breakfast?"

"Yes, we have a lovely breakfast, if you would like it." Brother John extended his hand and helped her to her feet. She had been completely unaware of the fact that she had slipped from her seat and was now kneeling. When she came to herself and noticed her position, she muttered, "What the...How did I get here?"

Brother John smiled again and gave a slight chuckle. "It happens all the time. I often find myself lying before the altar, not remembering how I got there."

"Well, it doesn't happen to me." And with that, she rose on her own and followed Brother John back out to the dining area where they had eaten last night. There, a complete breakfast buffet awaited them. She saw several of the monks eating heartily and carrying on animated conversations. She also saw Brandon at a table surrounded by several members of the order, chowing down a plate of eggs and waffles with a side of fruit. Wynona poured herself a cup of coffee, took a piece of toast, and sat in an empty seat at Brandon's table. The conversation was about Pete and the care and feeding of a Komodo dragon. Apparently one of the brothers had gone into the tool shed earlier that morning and was shocked to find Pete resting comfortably. Instead of being frightened, this monk—Brother Phil—was delighted to see up close such a fascinating creature and was anxious to speak to its owner. Brandon shared all that he had studied about the Komodo dragon and then shared how he had been led to it through his quest. Wynona cringed at this turn of the conversation. She fully expected the others to roll their eyes and lose interest, but to her surprise, the opposite happened. They were fascinated with Brandon's quest and saw it as a true venture into spirituality. Wynona listened with incredulity as the conversation turned, in her mind, bizarre. Then Brother Phil addressed Wynona.

"So, Wynona, what prompted you to go on this quest with Brandon?"

Wynona caught herself before she said what she wanted to say, and instead said that she was keeping a promise to her sister.

"And who is your sister?" Brother Phil inquired.

"Beth Swanson," Wynona replied. When she mentioned Beth, the brothers at the table became silent, and she could tell that the mention of her name touched them deeply.

Brother Phil then spoke. "We know and love your sister. She is in our prayers daily. You are blessed to have such a sister." As he spoke, the other brothers nodded their heads; some choked back tears.

Damn, Wynona thought. *Does everyone in the world know my sister?*

Brother Phil continued, "She often came to the monastery to deliver food, clothing, and other items that help us to do our work. We call her our little angel of mercy." The other brothers joined in her praise, commenting on her smile and her lovely singing voice, among other attributes. Then Brother Phil put his hand upon Wynona's and said, "She is a special child of God."

Wynona once more felt strong emotions stirring up within her as she tried to gain control of her anger. What she wanted to say was, "Then why the hell is God letting her die," but instead she excused herself and hurriedly made her way through the first door she could find. This door led her out onto the large patio overlooking the garden. She walked into the garden with the hopes of gaining some control over her volatile emotions. She ended up on a path that led through an archway covered by clinging vines and small flowers popping out from green leaves. She had walked a few more yards when she saw a small fountain and a stone seat facing a statue of a weeping woman who knelt in apparent agony. A small inscription at the base of the statue read, "Woman, why are you weeping?" Wynona had been brought up in church, and she knew the quote to be the words spoken to Mary Magdalene at the tomb of Jesus. Wynona couldn't really say how long she sat there on that bench—it could have been minutes, it could have been hours—for time seemed to cease for her as she pondered those words. She thought of all the reasons for her own weeping. She wept because of the loss of her father through the carelessness of others. She wept because she was losing the only person in her life who truly understood her. But more than that, she wept because she felt her life was a failure. She had worked so hard to escape her past hurts, but they seemed to chase her down, no matter how fast she ran. And then there were all the new hurts that had emerged to join in the chase. Her work was a series of deadlines and disappointments, and her relationships all seemed to end with angry breakups. She understood why Mary was weeping: the most important person in her life, the one who had promised her freedom from a life of futility, was dead. Of course, she was weeping. She had every right to weep. Suddenly, Wynona sensed that she was no longer alone and turned to see Brother John standing beside her. He had not said a word and would not have if she hadn't addressed him first.

"Seems like a perfect place for me—the statue of a weeping woman."

Brother John took a seat next to her on the bench. "Perfect in more ways than one, Wynona. Do you know your Bible?"

"It's been a while. Where I come from, it's not required reading."

He smiled and spoke gently. "Then let me remind you because it may give you some comfort. Mary was a woman who was on the wrong side of society, an outcast, a misfit, and she struggled with knowing her worth. So when Jesus called her to be one of his disciples, she found a new life and a new reason for living. Then the unimaginable happened—he was taken away from her by the cruelty of people. She thought her world had collapsed. Do you remember who said these words to her?"

Wynona did not answer but looked up at Brother John with pleading, tear-filled eyes. Brother John continued, "It was the risen Jesus, the very one she was weeping for."

Wynona brushed away her tears. "Kind of a dirty trick to play on her, don't you think?"

Brother John laughed. "I never thought of it that way. I thought it was rather playful of him. But I guess if you conquer death, you might just do something like that."

"Brother John, I don't mean to be disrespectful, but I don't see how any of that helps me."

Brother John then placed his hands tenderly on Wynona's wet cheeks. "Wynona, Jesus was saying to Mary, 'Your life is not over. It has just begun. Death is not the end. It is the beginning, and because I rose from the dead, I can bring you a new life, now and forever.' Child, I know you are in pain, and I don't have any easy answers for all that has happened to you. But I know that this same Jesus is ready to give you that message of hope, if you would be willing to receive it."

Wynona felt a flush of embarrassment and stood up. "I don't really know what Jesus did with her, but I know that it would take some kind of miracle to make me believe it was that simple."

Brother John also rose and looked with compassion on her. "The most profound truths *are* that simple, and I will ask God for that miracle."

"You do that, and while you're praying, pray that Beth doesn't die." Wynona then turned to leave. But before she could, Brother John reached out and put his hand upon her head.

"Gracious Father, show Wynona that she is not alone. Give her a message so she will know that there is hope beyond what she can see, a healing that is more powerful than death."

Wynona was speechless. She had never experienced someone so bold in their faith and yet so gentle in sharing it. Brother John could see that there was nothing more to say, so he changed the subject. "Brandon is collecting Pete and wants to start the return trip. Do you need anything for your journey?"

"A ride would be nice."

Again Brother John let loose a warm chuckle. "Well, I understand, but Brandon insists that his quest requires that he travel by foot. I, however, have given him directions that will make the journey a bit shorter, so you should be able to return to your cars by noon."

Wynona left the alcove and found the path that led to the shed where they had kept Pete for the night. As she drew closer, she noticed several monks standing in a circle around Brandon, asking him questions. Brandon was bending down, gently stroking Pete's snout, and answering every question as if he were a reptile expert. They were curious about the dragon's native habitat, how old Brandon thought he was, and what the plans were for his future.

"So, genius, what are you going to do with the world's largest reptile in Brandstad?"

Brandon looked up and saw Wynona pushing her way through the group of monks, and he smiled. "Well, I haven't quite figured that out, but we'll find a home for him when we get him back to the shelter."

"You do that. Let's go." Wynona began to walk in the direction she thought would lead her home but noticed that Brandon was not following. She stopped and barked back at him, "What's the problem now?"

Brandon gestured in another direction. "You're going the wrong way."

"Fine. Let's just get this quest over with." Wynona returned to Brandon, and they both started down a path that led out of the garden, through a grove of fruit trees, and up a rise to the plateau where they had stopped the night before. All the while, Pete seemed content in following Brandon. Wynona noticed this and commented, "For a big, fat lizard, he's pretty quick."

"Now there's no need to insult him. And for your information, Komodo dragons have been clocked at speeds of up to fifteen miles per hour, so yes, he could outrun you, if he wanted to."

Pete lifted his head, looked at Wynona, and stuck out his long, forked tongue. Wynona nervously eyed the big reptile and sighed. "That's comforting."

17
The Showdown

"IT'S A GREAT day to get me some dragon!" Connor stepped out of the car and strapped his sword and shield on his back. After adjusting his leather headband, he turned the side-view mirror around so he could admire his magnificence. "Too bad we can't bring our cell phones. I'd like to get a picture of me with its severed head."

Lisa yawned and shot a revolted look at Connor. "Relax, big man. Don't count your dragons before they're decapitated."

He then noticed Brandon's and Wynona's cars parked a short distance away. "Damn! We're late. That means we've got to get moving and kill it before that Twinkie makes it a pet."

"Why do we have to kill it? Maybe it's friendly," Kyle said as he collected his assortment of stuff from the trunk.

"There ain't no such thing as a friendly dragon. Besides, there's lots of reasons to get it. I've even heard that some people in China will pay big bucks for its teeth and stuff like that." Connor began to walk into the forest.

Lisa watched Connor begin down the path and then said in a matter-of-fact voice, "Hey, Hercules, you know where you're going?" Connor looked back with a sneer. "I think that thing, whatever it is, went that way." Lisa pointed toward the path that Brandon and

Wynona had taken the day before. Connor grunted, turned around, and took the path.

"Alliea, do you think today will be the day I use the Horn of Power?" Kyle asked sheepishly.

Lisa smiled warmly at Kyle. "Who knows? Could be." She headed out into the forest.

"Alliea?" Kyle trotted up to her side as they followed Connor. "It seems strange to be on this quest without Wanderer."

Lisa did not break her stride. "It was his decision. He could have stayed with us. He chose to go with her, and now he's against us."

"Why do we need to be against each other, couldn't we—"

Lisa stopped and turned to Kyle. "It is what it is. Let's go and see what happens. After all, that's what adventures are for." Kyle nodded, and all three of them followed the trail that disappeared into the thick overgrowth.

● ● ●

Steve finished his breakfast and stepped through the front door of Bill's. He was followed closely by Henry. In front of him was a motley assortment of city folk waiting for their instructions.

"We're all here, Mr. Poup, and Sally is rarin' to go." The hound bayed as the big, bearded farmer reached down to give it a pat on the head.

"Good, we'll need her." A rush of egotism flowed through Steve when he scanned the waiting crowd. "Now, we're not sure what we're dealing with out there..."

"Could be a dinosaur," Henry interrupted. He had fully recovered from the effects of the tranquilizer and was eager to find his piece of the glory.

Steve scowled at Henry. "We don't know that, but we do know it's big and can snap you in two, like a twig." The crowd reacted to Steve's comment with a combination of awe and excitement.

Another burly man, who was wielding a shotgun, shouted from the crowd. "So what are we going to do when we find it?"

Speaking in his most authoritative voice, Steve said, "Well, Harper, that depends on if we can successfully capture it."

Harper scowled. "I didn't bring my shotgun to capture this thing. I'm going to blow it back to wherever it came from!" A roar of approval came from the posse, which was quickly morphing into something more like a lynch mob.

Attempting to calm the crowd, Steve said, "It may come to that if I can't tranquilize it."

Then another voice rose above the din. "Yeah, like you did Henry there." Suddenly the angry clamor turned into laughter, and the facade of Steve's authority quickly vanished.

Attempting to regain his dignity, Steve raised his voice. "Never mind that. When we get to Old Man Stealy's place, I want everyone to stay together and be ready for anything. Any questions?" There was no response from the crowd. "Then mount up!" The townspeople loaded themselves into an assortment of pickups and ATVs that bore a striking resemblance to a hillbilly parade, complete with music blaring, people shouting, and dogs barking.

• • •

Brother John's directions led Brandon and Wynona up upon the ridge that paralleled the stream and then through several small valleys where rivulets cut through the forest to join the larger stream. Pete was content with following Brandon to the point that it seemed unnecessary to have him on a leash.

Brandon stopped at one of the small streams to get a drink of water. "I wonder how Old Man Stealy was able to train Pete so well. He seems practically domesticated. You know, the London zoo has a couple of Komodos that they have trained, but they would think this was uncanny."

Wynona looked down at Pete, who was sharing a drink with Brandon. "I must admit that you two make a cute couple. I can even see the family resemblance."

Brandon stood up. "I know you're joking, but there's something about him that makes me think we're not so different."

"Let me guess...dental hygiene? No? Are you both into eating rotting animal carcasses? OK, I give up. How are you two alike?"

"We're both out of our element. He's from an exotic island in Indonesia and has somehow found himself in a world of mountains, pine trees, and snow, and I—well, I have never felt completely comfortable among the culture I came from. Pete belongs back on his island, and I belong...I guess I'm not really sure where I belong."

Wynona's voice softened. With a hint of a smile, she said, "Then I guess we have that in common too."

Brandon continued, "I gotta say that I felt like I was at home with Brother John and the other brothers. They seem to have found something that I wish I had. Did you feel it too?"

Wynona looked at the ground and tried to put into words what she had felt, but all she managed to say was, "He was very kind to us."

"Wynona, when we get back, what are you going to do?"

"Do?"

"Are you going back to that city job?"

"Why wouldn't I?"

"I don't know. I was just wondering if you were thinking that there might be a better place for you." Brandon stooped down again and scratched Pete behind his ear. "You didn't seem very happy when you came here, and I was thinking that some of that was because of where you've been."

Wynona didn't know what to say. She was feeling like all that had happened to her since she'd come back to Brandstad was a terrible dream, but now she wondered if the terrible dream was actually the life she'd been pursuing. She wanted to say she was confused and full of contradictory feelings, but instead she, once again, put on her cloak of invulnerability and simply responded to Brandon's insights with, "I think we'd better get going now."

Brandon could see that no more was going to be said on the subject, so he gave Pete one last pat and headed out on the trail. The two kept their thoughts to themselves, but all along the trail, the words of Brother John's prayer about hope beyond what she could see burrowed deeper and deeper into Wynona's soul.

• • •

Connor stopped on the trail. "There's no telling what direction they went. We could be heading the wrong way for all we know."

Lisa pulled up behind him. "Then I think our best bet is to go back to the cars and wait for them there."

Connor didn't want to admit it, but that was the only way he would be sure to confront Brandon, and he was far more eager to pick a fight with Brandon than he was to traipse endlessly through the woods.

"OK, but when we find them, you let me handle the wizard."

Lisa was already turned around and heading back to the Stealy house when she shouted her response over her shoulder. "Done."

• • •

The caravan of pickup trucks and other assorted vehicles arrived in a cloud of dust in front of Old Man Stealy's house. Steve stepped out of his truck and took a stance. Henry then put an assortment of animal-catching equipment on him, like a squire would put the armor on a knight. Steve spread his legs and put his hands on his hips in a Patton-like pose while the crowd of scruffy characters gathered around him. Then he held up his arms for quiet.

"Now we're going out there to face something that's so horrible you may not be able to tell your children for fear of causing them great psychological harm. Some of you may be lost in this great struggle, but I say to the rest of you who survive, push on...All true Americans love a fight...and when you reach over to wipe the dirt from your face and find it's the blood and guts from what used to be your neighbor standing next to you, then you'll know what to do. We're going out there like crap through a goose; we're going to grab that thing by its neck—if it has a neck—and kick it in the butt all the way back to Brandstad!"

The crowd grew silent. For the first time, they realized there might be some danger in what they were about to do—not that they hadn't done foolish things before, but those things were usually done under the influence of alcohol. Since it was early, the bars had not yet opened, and the courage of the bottle was not in play.

The burly man was the first to speak. "I didn't sign up to have my guts sprayed on Harper here."

Harper spoke up. "Me neither. I say we meet tonight at the Tree Hugger and discuss this over a few beers. After all, that thing out there hasn't done me any harm." The energy of the crowd began to dissipate, and one by one, they slowly retreated to their vehicles.

Steve, sensing his moment of glory was fading, began to plead. "What? Wait! We've got a job to do. We're going to save our city."

Harper had climbed into the cab of his truck as Steve stood by his window.

"But we were going to get this thing together!"

Harper's truck roared to life, and he turned to look at the now disheartened Steve. "You're the professional. You're getting paid to do this, so go do it."

Henry, oblivious to the group dynamic, excitedly approached Steve. "Which way, General?"

Steve was disgusted by the turn in his fortunes. "What, are you crazy? I'm not going out there alone. That thing's dangerous!"

• • •

The LARPers emerged from the forest while the posse was return-ing to their vehicles. Kyle was the first to see them. "What's going on over there?"

Lisa looked in the direction of the crowd. "Looks like we're not the only ones hunting the dragon."

Not willing to let anyone spoil his conquest, Connor sprang to action. "I'll be damned if they're going to get it before I do." He sprinted to where the townspeople were still preparing to leave and shouted. "I am Perales the Proud, and nobody gets my dragon unless they come through me."

The effect on the crowd was not what Connor was hoping for. They burst out in laughter, and someone yelled, "Hey, Connor, does your dad know you're running around in the forest like some kind of whacked-out weirdo?"

Connor retorted, "Maybe you won't think I'm so weird when I run my sword through your belly." With this, Connor unsheathed his weapon.

Unfortunately for Connor, the man who had made the comment had prepared himself for something a lot more dangerous than a sword. "Whoa there, boy. You might want to say hi to Mr. Twelve Gauge before you start swinging that oversized pocket knife." Connor thought better of the confrontation and slowly put his sword away.

Knowing Connor's propensity for foolish behavior, Lisa and Kyle rushed into the crowd. The shock of seeing the three LARPers in full attire created a cascade of laughter throughout the crowd. Harper had stepped out of his truck when he saw the strange trio approach-ing. "Looks like the woods are full of crazies!" He turned to his friend with the hound. "Hey, sic Sally on them."

Lisa attempted to defuse the situation. "OK, boys, looks like we're after the same thing, so let's not get testy."

Steve was still nursing his bruised ego but found hope in Lisa's comment. "Did you see it?"

"No, we're hoping that some others did and that we'd meet them here."

"So there are more of you out there?"

The timing was poor for Brandon, Wynona, and Pete as they emerged from the forest.

Harper was the first to see them. "What the hell?"

Connor turned to see what Harper was looking at, and when he saw the trio emerging from the forest, he shouted, "Yes!"

Steve spied Pete obediently being led by Brandon and turned to Henry. "Is that it?"

Henry just shrugged his shoulders. "It looked a lot bigger."

Connor moved quickly toward Brandon. "So you've brought me the dragon. Thanks!" Connor unsheathed his sword and charged at Pete, ready to take a swipe at his enormous head. Brandon stepped in front of Pete, grasping his staff with both hands.

Wynona screamed and quickly took a position beside Brandon. "Hold on, boys. Can't you settle your differences some other way?"

Connor waved his sword, and the blade cut the air with a swoosh. "There ain't no other way. That's the thing that's been causing all the trouble, and I'm going to take its head off!"

Wynona, still attempting to bring sanity to an unreal situation, spoke low and slow, but there was a fearful edge to her words. "Settle down, Connor. You've got a sword, and all Brandon has is a stick—not much of a fair fight, I'd say."

Connor continued to wave his sword about, narrowly missing both Wynona and Brandon. "Then tell him to step aside and he won't get hurt, because I'm going to kill that thing."

Brandon nudged Wynona to one side and stepped forward to block Connor's path. "Then you're going to have to come through me."

"With pleasure." Connor took a swipe at Brandon, who parried his blow so that the sword fell harmlessly into the dirt. Brandon then swiftly struck at Connor's feet, which sent him flying.

"You still haven't learned how to stay on your feet, have you, Perales?"

Connor quickly arose, picked up his sword, and gritted his teeth. "Let's see how well you handle that stick with a few less fingers." He brought his sword down on Brandon's staff and splintered it into two pieces.

Wynona, seeing that things were getting serious again, appealed for reason. "Hey, let's put down the toys and talk."

Connor knew he had the advantage, so he pressed his attack. "Talking's over. It's time for some slaying."

Brandon nimbly wielded the two sticks so that every time Connor swiped at him with his sword, Brandon deftly struck several numbing blows at his joints, which slowed his reactions. Connor groaned in pain, but he was nothing if not persistent. He would take a hack at Brandon and then receive several sharp blows without any means of defending against them, so that eventually his arms became so numb he was not able to hold onto his weapon. At this point, any rational person would have accepted defeat, but not Connor. When skill failed him, as it usually did, he always reverted to his basic football tactics. Though he didn't have the talent necessary to be a quarterback, he was strong and determined, and he called up all the tackling training he'd learned over years of football practice.

"OK, if that's how you want to play this game, then let's do this another way." Connor put his head down and rushed Brandon, driving him to the ground, where they began to wrestle in the dirt while the others helplessly looked on.

Wynona screamed at Lisa. "Do something!"

Lisa casually lit a cigarette and took a puff. "Let 'em wear themselves out. It will do them good."

Meanwhile, unnoticed by the group, Sheriff Joe's squad car rolled up and parked behind Wynona's car. When he saw the rumble, he turned on his lights and punched the siren a few times. Wynona glanced up, as did the rest of the group, and saw Sheriff Joe exit his car and walk toward the pair of men, who were still rolling around on the ground, oblivious to the sheriff's presence.

"When you boys are through, I need to say something." He glanced down at Pete. "Whoa, what's that?"

Wynona calmly stated, "That's Pete. He's a Komodo dragon."

"So that's what's been causing all the fuss. Doesn't look too dangerous to me."

Brandon and Connor, finally realizing just how silly they looked, got up and began to dust themselves off.

Brandon spoke up in defense of the dragon. "He's not dangerous, unless you're a hunk of rotting meat, so back off. He's done nothing except to be in the wrong place with the wrong people."

Sheriff Joe looked intently at Pete, who was wagging his head back and forth. "OK, nobody's going to hurt him. Just get him out of the forest so we can put all these stupid rumors to rest." He then went over to Pete and began to admire the giant lizard.

Wynona ran over to Brandon. "I thought you were going to get chopped up. Where did you learn to fight like that?"

Brandon was still catching his breath. "I joined the army after you left and learned a few useful skills, like escrima, the Filipino art of fighting sticks."

"I didn't know you joined the army." Wynona was becoming more interested in this man who had made such a transformation from what she had remembered him to be.

"Yeah, and I also got my degree in biology so that I could become a vet. That's why I came back to Brandstad, to earn enough money to go back to school."

She looked at Brandon as if seeing him for the first time. "You've got a degree? Brandon, you amaze me."

Brandon cracked a smile. "Well, that's something I haven't seen— Wynona amazed."

Sheriff Joe turned back to the group. "Wynona, I came out here to find you."

"Me?"

"You've got to go home. I'm sorry to say it, but Beth has taken a turn for the worse, and you need to get back right now."

Wynona didn't hesitate but sprinted to her car and tore down the dirt road toward town. Everyone else stopped and stared at one another, realizing just how foolish their own little quarrel had been when faced with the impending death of someone they all knew and cared deeply about.

Connor was the first to speak. "What's a Komodo dragon?"

Brandon went over to Pete and began to scratch behind his ear. "He's the largest reptile in the world."

Sheriff Joe took off his hat. "That's one helluva lizard!"

Kyle had been hanging back during the fight, and he now stepped forward. "Sheriff, how's Beth?"

Sheriff Joe became serious. "Doc says she's probably not going to make it through the night." All of them became quiet, and Kyle began to weep silently. Lisa went over to the little dwarf and held him as he cried on her breast.

Brandon broke the silence. "Come on, Pete. We'd better get you to the shelter."

Connor, for all his bluster, was also deeply affected by the news. He felt a sensation that was new to him—shame. "Need any help?"

Brandon was surprised by the offer but also saw it as an attempt to repair their relationship, which he was willing to accept. "I could use some help getting him in the Jeep. He's quite a load."

While Brandon and Connor walked Pete to the Jeep, Sheriff Joe turned to Steve, Henry, and the rest of the posse. "All of you, get back in your vehicles and go home before I arrest you for trespassing." Then he got back in his squad car and headed back to town, which left Kyle and Lisa alone.

"Lisa, do you suppose if I blew the Horn of Power now, it would help Beth?"

Lisa held Kyle affectionately. "I don't know, Kyle. I just don't know. Let's go with Brandon and Connor and talk about it. Looks like we're back together again, and we should make that decision together." The two of them joined Brandon and Connor, who had just lifted Pete into the Jeep. They huddled for a few moments and then returned to their cars and headed down the dirt road toward Brandstad.

18
Beth's Homegoing

WYNONA'S THOUGHTS RACED as fast as her car as she sped toward town. She thought about all the adventures she'd had with her sister and the secrets they'd shared together that no one else would ever know. She wondered what happened to secrets when the one you've kept them with dies. Do they disappear with the person or do they linger until there is no one left to remember them? Somehow, it seemed inconceivable that someone would live a full life, rich with experiences, and there would be nothing left when he or she died. She then remembered all the gravestones in the cemetery with their epitaphs of, "Loving husband and father," or "We will always remember." She wondered if anyone did remember, and if not, what was left of the person who was becoming dust beneath those well-intentioned testimonials. Would Beth's fate be the same as all the others? Wynona found it too horrible to think about. She couldn't let her mind wander into those dark valleys, because if she did, she was not sure she would ever come out. What she would do was take each day, one hour, one minute, and one second at a time. Her only goal right then was to be with Beth while she could.

Her mind then turned to self-condemnation. *Why did I out on that stupid quest with Brandon when Beth is so sick? But didn't Beth almost order me to go? So if I don't get home in time, it's Beth's fault, right?*

These and other thoughts flooded Wynona's mind as she drove the familiar streets of Brandstad. Then her thoughts found a new focus. *Do you suppose that wherever Beth is going that she will see Father? Could it be possible that they will be together again?* Then the rational Wynona stepped in to answer. *Dead is dead, and that's all there is to it. I don't need to believe in some afterlife to live.* But Beth believed, and Wynona wondered if maybe believing was all that mattered. For a brief moment, she weighed the logic behind this line of reasoning: "If I believe and it is not true, then I don't lose anything. But if I don't believe and it is true, then I have lost everything." *Don't be ridiculous,* she told herself. *How can you live believing in something that you don't know is true? What kind of life is that?* Then a voice came from out of nowhere. She almost turned around to see if someone else was in the car. It said, "What about the life Beth has been living? See how so many people love her. Notice the joy she has even when she's in such pain. Wasn't that a life worth living?"

About this time, Wynona found herself pulling up in front of her home. She sat in the car for a few moments and prepared herself to experience something she was not ready to face. Her heart was racing, and her senses seemed to be narrowly focused on the one thing she knew she must do—go to Beth. She walked up the steps without feeling the ground and opened the door to see her mother and the doctor standing outside of Beth's room. June ran up to Wynona and wrapped her arms around her.

"I'm so glad you're here. The doctor said it could be any time now, and I know that Beth wanted you to be with her." Wynona could not speak but simply nodded and walked the few paces to Beth's room. The door was open, and she could see Beth there, unresponsive and breathing shallowly. She entered the room and sat down on the chair next to the bed and placed her hand on Beth's. It felt cold but not yet lifeless. Wynona didn't speak; she didn't know what to say. All she could do was rest her head on the side of the bed and listen to Beth's slow, shallow breathing.

She then felt a hand upon her shoulder; it was June. "She left you a note in case you came when she was no longer able to speak. It's there on her Bible."

Wynona looked at the nightstand and saw a little yellow piece of paper on top of the Bible. She reached for the note, then sat back on the chair and opened it, but her eyes were too full of tears to focus on the words. She wiped her tears on her sleeve and began to read.

Dear Darling Wynona,

If you're reading this, it's because I'm not able to talk. But you know a thing like dying won't shut me up. I know that you're probably confused and even angry right now, and I don't blame you. Frankly, I don't understand why I need to go away so soon either. There's so much I would've liked to do, not to mention seeing all the great things you are going to do. But I put those decisions into the hands of the one who knows all things. Right now, you're probably having a hard time knowing what to do. You always want to know what to do on every occasion, so I'm going to help you here. I would like you to take my Bible and read it to me now. I know that you don't know what to read, so I'm going to make this simple. Just open it up, and read wherever your eyes land. I know it will be the perfect place. I love you, I will always love you, and I will be waiting for you in a place where there are no more tears, no more pain, and where joy will be undiminished. Dad and I will greet you, and we'll all be together again. Who knows? Maybe we'll even chase some heavenly butterflies together. Love, Beth.

Whether it was out of shock or denial, Wynona began to have a playful conversation with Beth. "It's just like you to make a Sunday school lesson out of your death." She took the Bible and said, "Hey, what if I land on one of those begat sections. That would teach you." Wynona opened the Bible, and it fell to Song of Songs, chapter 2. Wynona couldn't help but smile because, even though it had been years, she remembered the days when she would sit in the back of the church with other adolescent dissidents and snicker over this particular book's allusions to women's breasts being like ripe fruit. "OK, Beth, you always know best. See if you can get out of this one." She began to read.

> Listen! My beloved!
> Look! Here he comes,
> leaping across the mountains,
> bounding over the hills.
> My beloved is like a gazelle or a young stag.
> Look! There he stands behind our wall,
> gazing through the windows,
> peering through the lattice.
> My beloved spoke and said to me,
> "Arise, my darling,
> my beautiful one, come with me.
> See! The winter is past;
> the rains are over and gone.
> Flowers appear on the earth;
> the season of singing has come,
> the cooing of doves
> is heard in our land.
> The fig tree forms its early fruit;
> the blossoming vines spread their fragrance.
> Arise, come, my darling;
> my beautiful one, come with me."

As she read, Wynona was struck with the very real sense that this was a personal message to Beth and that she was being swept up by an eternal lover who had come to take his beloved with him. When she came to the last line, a glow came over Beth's face, and a smile broke out like Wynona had seen a thousand times before. But this one was even more sweet and filled with expectation. Then Wynona noticed Beth's breathing had stopped, and the room became completely silent. Beth was gone.

June let out a moan and clung to Wynona, but to Wynona's surprise, there was no explosive emotional display, only simple and uncomplicated grief. Wynona looked back at Beth and had an overpowering feeling that she was no longer there. The body remained, but the essence of the reality of Beth had left. And then the thought again entered her mind, *Where did she go?* The words she had read echoed in her like a shout in a canyon, "Come with me." Wynona wondered, *Did someone take Beth? Is there a place where the "winter is past"?*

The hours following Beth's death were a blur. Wynona mostly retreated to her room and shunned visits from well-meaning people. She found herself looking through boxes of photographs of her sister. What she saw made her smile, cry, laugh, and be angry. When she did sleep, which was infrequently, it was fitful and filled with dreams of fire and open graves. There really was no comfort for Wynona, not in looking at the past and definitely not in thinking of the future.

Beth's funeral was set for Tuesday, and Wynona decided to leave town directly after the burial. Although she was not excited about returning to her normal life, she determined she didn't have any other life to return to.

The weekend seemed interminable, but at last it mercifully dissolved into Monday, which was spent like the other days—attempting to avoid people and trying desperately to keep her mind off the hopelessness that haunted her. Finally, night came, and she thought, *Just one more day, and I can leave this place.* She packed her bags, leaving out only what she would wear to the funeral, and put them in the trunk of her car. June had prepared a light dinner, and they sat together sharing quiet moments of memories of Beth.

During a pause in their conversation, June reached over to Wynona and took her hand. "Please don't be worried about me. I have so many friends that I expect I'm going to need to get an appointment secretary."

Wynona was a little taken aback by her mother's comment, partly because this was not the clinging, needy mother she had known, but even more so because she had not really considered staying and caring for her grieving mother. In fact, she had not really considered anyone else's grief but her own. She managed a smile at her mother's sincerity and said, "Thank you." The fact was that June was dealing with the death of her oldest daughter better than Wynona. June was able to cry and had accepted the comfort of numerous friends who had visited in the few days after Beth's passing. As a testimony to their love, the kitchen counter was cluttered with all sorts of baked goods, and the refrigerator was stuffed with casseroles. No, it was Wynona who would go back to a life where no one would know or care that Beth had died.

After dinner, Wynona helped with the dishes and assisted June in packaging some of the excess food so that she could drop it off to others in need. Before Wynona left for her bedroom, June put her arms around her and gave her a tender kiss on the cheek.

"Well, sweetie, I guess it's just you and me now. I know that you don't like living here and that you've made your own life for yourself, but I want you to know this will always be your home and that wherever in this world you go, you are deeply and sincerely loved."

Wynona's face flushed, and she felt an overwhelming desire to say that she wasn't going anywhere, that she had decided to stay in Brandstad. But of course that was not going to happen. Wynona had worked too hard to throw it all away and live in some backwoods town. But the knowledge that there would always be a place to return to if everything else in her world came crashing down was an unforeseen comfort.

Back in her room, Wynona prepared for her last night in Brandstad and sincerely hoped it would be a restful one. As she lay on her bed, she thought through all the events of the past week. Again, the hopelessness of the situation nearly tore her soul in two. If only there was something that would prove there was more to it than being put into the ground with a few kind words. And then Wynona prayed. It was not the kind of prayer she had learned in Sunday school with the predictable formula of formal words. It was more of a heart pleading, directed toward a God she did not know and was not even sure she wanted to know. It was in response to Father John's prayer for hope and the starry night full of wonder on the hilltop. It was prompted by the heart and smile of her dear sister and incited by the mystery of the stained-glass windows in the chapel. And most of all, it was just a simple pleading of one whose heart was breaking. "God, if you are real, if there is more to this life, let me know. Show me." Wynona prayed this prayer, not knowing what would happen but hoping that something would. But the room was silent, and there were no signs or wonders. "So that's your answer? Then that settles it." Wynona pulled the covers up around her neck, and for the first time since she could remember, she fell into a dreamless sleep.

She awoke the next morning, dressed, and walked down the stairs to the tomblike silence of the house. She couldn't even bear to turn toward Beth's room but went straight to her car and headed for the church. Wynona still planned to leave directly from the burial and once again be swallowed up in the life of meetings, deadlines, and ambition. The morning of Beth's funeral was clear with a crisp northerly wind that felt more like early spring than early summer. The church was packed, with overflow chairs set up in the narthex. Visitation was in the church's parlor and preceded the service by two hours. Wynona dutifully stood by her mother and accepted the condolences of Beth's friends. They all said such kind things about Beth and spoke with genuine affection and deep emotion. More than one person approached June and Wynona and without uttering a word, simply put out their hands as if they were somehow going to pull them out of the water onto dry land. Brother John and the other monks from the monastery came too. Their presence was more felt than heard because somehow just their way of being gave off a peculiar sense of comfort. Brother John greeted Wynona with a few kind words, but it wasn't his words that most impressed her. He looked intently into her face with an almost irreverent twinkle in his eyes that unsettled her. It was almost as if he had a secret he was bursting to tell her but knew he couldn't. Brandon and the other LARPers were also there, but thankfully, they were not costumed.

Brandon clasped Wynona's hand with great tenderness. "Thank you for going with me to look for Pete. I know it was a sacrifice."

"Yeah, well, Beth wanted me to go, so I guess I really did it for her."

This was all Brandon had time to say to Wynona, though there were a great many other things he would like to have said, but the receiving line was long, and it was not the time or place. Kyle placed himself in front of Wynona and stood awkwardly for several moments before Lisa nudged him on. When Lisa's turn came, she was quiet and direct.

"Beth was simply the kindest, most godly person I have ever known, and the world will be a poorer place now that she is gone."

Wynona was stunned by this statement coming from the most notorious bad girl of Brandstad, but she was realizing that there was so much more to Beth's short life than she ever knew. Wynona nodded in acknowledgment. The next person in line was Connor. The big man stood sheepishly in front of Wynona and searched for words. He had been rehearsing what to say while waiting in line and had finally decided on something that was said to him at his grandfather's funeral. What he wanted to say was, "I am very sorry for your loss," but when he actually stood in front of Wynona and June, he said what was truly on his heart. "She gave me hot chocolate when I was cold." He was a bit shocked and dismayed that he hadn't said the more appropriate statement, but somehow, it was a far more meaningful and comforting sentiment.

June smiled at the uncomfortable young man standing before her and said, "Well, that's what Jesus would do, so I guess that's why Beth did it." This again gave Wynona pause. She noticed her mother's confident strength and marveled. She thought that either she had completely misjudged her mother over the years, or somehow the ordeal of witnessing the death of her oldest daughter had made her into another person. In that split second, she realized that there really was a deep confidence in June during this time of grief that was nothing like what she herself was experiencing. She wished she could have that peace but knew she was not like her mother. Faith had come easily to June and Beth but not to her. She couldn't make that leap into the unknown without some kind of proof. That was really what she had been praying for last night, and it had not been given to her.

The service was a touching tribute to a short life lived well. There were some songs performed by the same group she had seen at the Tree Hugger only a few nights before, and once again, Wynona marveled at how Beth's life reached such a varied group of people. The elementary school choir sang one of Beth's favorite songs—the same one she had heard Beth listening to in her room. Wynona read from a passage in John where Jesus was comforting Martha after the death of her brother, Lazarus, with the words, "I am the resurrection and the life. He who believes in me though he were dead yet shall he live." But even these words fell upon the hard soil of Wynona's bitter heart. Finally, Pastor Thomas gave a short message that Wynona didn't hear, and the service ended.

Several men came to the head of the church and walked alongside the casket as it was rolled down the aisle to the front of the church, where they stopped and picked it up, three on each side. The church was a throwback to the early settler days, and so it sat adjacent to the cemetery. The men walked the coffin the short distance to the grave site, and the congregation filed in an orderly procession behind them with the pastor leading the way, followed by June and Wynona. They followed a narrow road that took them to the place along the hillside where Wynona's father was buried. There they placed the coffin above a freshly dug grave. Chairs were positioned in front of the grave for June and Wynona, and the rest of the attendees stood in concentric circles around them. Pastor Thomas said a few more words of which Wynona caught only a few lines.

Wynona's thoughts were on the futility of the strange thing called life—how we struggle when we live it, and how we grieve when it is over. There always seemed to be the hunger for what was next—the next relationship, the next job, the climbing to the top of the heap, and the slow, agonizing descent when we are too tired to stay. And finally, Wynona realized, we all end up like Beth, in a hole in the ground or having our ashes spread over some beloved part of the world. Wynona's hopelessness was not complete; there was still a spark of something that she couldn't call hope, but there was a little part of her that was skeptical of her skepticism. It was a small part indeed, and there was precious little to fan its tiny spark into a flame.

Pastor Thomas said a few more words, and then it was time to lower the casket. A small white table with two red roses had been placed at the head of the casket, and June and Wynona stood and slowly walked up to the table, took the roses, and prepared to toss them onto the casket as it was being lowered into the earth. They took their places, and one of the pallbearers began to crank the lever that caused the coffin to slowly descend. June tossed her rose and returned to her seat. Wynona was prepared to toss her rose, but something stopped her. She stood motionless above the coffin while holding her rose over the open grave, but she couldn't let go of it. It was as if something had grasped her hand and held it there suspended, unable to let go of the rose but equally unable to be retracted. She looked helplessly at Pastor Thomas and then turned to her mother, mouthing the words, "I can't move." Then, at the top of the hill, Wynona saw figures emerging from behind the crest. It was Connor, Kyle, Lisa, and finally Brandon, appearing in full LARP splendor. All eyes were on Wynona, and when her eyes became fixed on the foursome, everyone else turned to look at them as well.

The four stood at the top of the hill looking down on the grave-side service and Kyle glanced up at Brandon. "Now?"

Brandon smiled down at the little dwarf. "Yes, now." Kyle removed the Horn of Power from his shoulder and prepared to blow into it.

"You do know how to blow that thing, don't you?" Lisa asked with a frozen smile on her face. Even she was feeling a little exposed to public ridicule.

Kyle said innocently, "I don't know. I've never done this before."

Connor groaned. "Great, we're all going to have to move to another town after this."

Brandon put his hand on Kyle's shoulder. "Brummel, of the clan of Ancient Mountain Dwarves, this is your token. Blow!"

Kyle straightened up to his full height, put the Horn of Power to his lips, and blew with all his might. What came out could only be compared to the sound a dying goose being run over by a car. It was loud but hardly triumphant. Connor's face turned red, and he could barely manage to keep himself from escaping by sprinting back down the hill. Lisa took it a bit more in stride and muttered, "So what did you expect, Wynton Marsalis?"

The last dying echo of the horn reverberated in the valley, and then there was silence.

Kyle whispered to Brandon, "So what happens now?"

"Darned if I know," Brandon replied.

The reaction from the funeral attendees was mixed. There were those who were appalled at such a foolish display and thought it sac-rilegious. And there were those who began to outwardly chuckle at the utter absurdity of the LARPers' deed. Brother John looked on admiringly at the bold group of LARPers and thought it a completely appropriate tribute. Wynona didn't really know what to think. She was still stuck in her frozen state and was wondering if she would need help returning to her seat. After what seemed like an eternity, the crowd began to nervously shuffle their feet. Some wondered why Wynona was waiting so long to go back to her seat. The man who was lowering the coffin had finished his job and was confused by the failure to stick to the script.

Pastor Thomas was about to begin ad-libbing when there came a slight puff of wind, barely noticeable. A warm southerly breeze had begun—very gentle but very distinct. Then something amazing happened. A single monarch butterfly appeared above the graveside gathering and flitted just above their heads. It almost landed upon several people before it floated its way over to Wynona and with perfect adeptness landed upon her outstretched rose. Wynona stared with astonishment as it perched upon her flower and looked back at her. It was then that she found she had use of her hand again, but instead of dropping the flower on the casket, she brought it back and held it close to her face, looking intently into the eyes of the butterfly and half expecting it to speak to her. Instead, it cheerily flapped its wings for another few moments and then headed off into the sky. The heads of all the mourners also tracked the butterfly's ascent with rapt attention.

"Was that the miracle?" Kyle asked as he put his horn back over his shoulder.

Brandon was still gazing at Wynona and the butterfly. "Don't know. Maybe."

Wynona did not take her eyes off the butterfly as it began to fly off into the distance, nor did the rest of the group of mourners. She was about to return to her seat when she noticed that the place where the butterfly had disappeared was becoming strangely foggy. There was something odd happening in that part of the sky that didn't fit any category of natural phenomena she knew. The fog was growing larger, and swirled and undulated in multiple patterns and colors. It grew closer and closer until it came over the group like waves washing upon the shore. The colored cloud consisted of thousands upon thousands of butterflies filling the air with their soft, exquisite beauty. They darted in and out of the onlookers and landed in bunches upon outstretched fingers and arms. Laughter and spontaneous applause rose from what, moments before, had been mourners. They had been transformed into celebrators. Wynona forgot all her grief and sadness and danced with the butterflies, just like she had when she and Beth were little girls. Though the focus was on the tsunami of butterflies, if anyone had looked up to the top of the hill, they would have seen an equally remarkable sight. The foursome laughed and hugged one another and sealed a mystical bond that would last a lifetime. Even Brandon and Connor, as different as they were, would go on to become dear friends, each adding to the other's life in powerful ways.

Beth's funeral was the most unusual event in the history of Brandstad. Some attempted to explain it through the movement of wind currents and atmospheric conditions, but everyone there knew that it was a miraculous event produced by an extraordinary life.

Wynona's life was forever changed that day, but as with most change, it was both sudden and gradual. The day of the butterflies—or so it was called by all the townspeople—affected Wynona profoundly by creating a small crack in the door of her heart, which had been closed ever since the death of her father. It was strange that the death of a loved one could produce such a healing, but so it was with Wynona, and it began with a single butterfly perching upon her hand. When the cloud of butterflies descended upon the mourners, Wynona had felt the lifting of an invisible weight, and a flush of lightness had swept over her. She felt a peace she couldn't recall ever having experienced before. But Wynona was determined to never be held back, and Brandstad still epitomized a lifestyle that she abhorred. She was resolute. She would never return except for brief visits. Her life was in the city where she would find the success she longed for. She stayed with the plan and began the twelve-hour drive back to the city and her future.

But this was not the same Wynona that had left the city a week earlier. Those things that had been so important to her—her status, the money, even the upwardly mobile boyfriends—were losing their grip upon her soul, like melting snow on a warm spring day. Every mile closer to the city led to an imperceptible rise in the temperature of her heart, melting the solid ice block of resentment and anger that had encased her soul for so many years. She came within sight of the city and could see the massive skyscrapers that had formerly risen up to beckon her but which now were silent and foreboding. They stood like colossal tombstones in a place that offered only death. For the first time, she could not remember why she was so eager to return to her old life. "I was miserable here!" she shouted. The sound of her voice shocked her as much as the categorical nature of the truth she proclaimed. She was miserable in her job and with her friends and in the life that she had worked so hard to create. Yet where was she to go? Brandstad? No! That was not the answer. But where?

There is a perilous moment in the life of one who has seen a new and better way but is still held in the power of the former life. It's as if the prison doors have swung open to allow the captive to leave, but the life of a prisoner, as terrible as it is, seems better than the unknown life of freedom. Wynona was in that moment. She knew there had been a change in her. She was seeing more clearly now than she had ever seen. She saw that Beth's brief life had a weight to it that far exceeded its length. If she could capture a small piece of the happiness that Beth had, she would never want for anything else. She saw that though the LARPers were exceedingly strange and that Brandon's ambitions were incomprehensible, there was something beautiful about a quest that had produced such a conclusion. And what about that dragon? Who would have guessed that she would be party to saving the life of such a creature? But even more absurd, who would have thought that such a ridiculous creature could be an instrument in bringing her life? And who could have foreseen that her prayer would be answered in a way she never, ever expected?

These were questions Wynona could not answer. The lesson had not yet been fully learned. But this time, she was deciding to run to, instead of away from, her pain. Suddenly, a strange and unique compulsion came over her. Caught up in her thoughts, her driving had been automatic. She took no notice of anything but the road that stretched out before her. Now she had an intense desire to turn around and go back to Brandstad. As if waking from a dream, she looked out of her windshield and saw the sign: Brandstad, 60 miles. Had she been returning home all this time and never realized it? When did she turn around? She didn't remember. But her questions were replaced by a flood of peace that overcame her as she continued down the highway and eventually turned up a small paved driveway that led to the abbey where she had stayed only a few days before. This time, she was there for more than the comfort of a bed and a meal; she was there to find her soul.

It was morning when she arrived, and the sun had risen so that the house and gardens were awash in brilliant light. The grounds were empty, so she wandered back to the garden, and as if magnetically drawn, she came to the statue of Mary Magdalene and read again the inscription: "Woman, why are you weeping?" The petite red-and-white flowers clung to the stone bench, and she sat in silence. She had lived this all before, but this time, new and exciting thoughts entered her mind. *What if life doesn't end in death? What if the question was not a rebuke or a cruel joke but an opportunity for Mary to open her mind to a new reality? And what if the answer that Mary received was the same for me?* Death had robbed Wynona of the two most precious people in her life, but she wondered if there were something greater than death, something that transcended the grave. Beth loved the butterflies because they were beautiful, but she loved them even more because they were a symbol of going from the state of a lowly caterpillar to a soaring butterfly. Wynona wondered if death could be coming to the end of one existence to make way for something new that was beyond her understanding. If not, then why all those butterflies? Her tears began to flow, but this time, they were not tears of pain but tears of healing. For the first time, she was stepping out of the cold cell where her heart had been locked away. She was stepping into the fresh, sweet air of hope.

Wynona raised her eyes and saw Brother John looking down on her with compassion. He held out his hand and with a gentle voice said, "So, my dear Wynona, why are you crying?"

Through her tears, she reached up and took his hand. "For joy. This time it's for joy."

Author Biography

A passionate and gifted author, James C. Tillman draws his readers closer to God through his compelling stories and ignites their desire to know truth through his stirring insights. In addition to writing and producing numerous plays and films, he has recently completed the Kingdom Chronicles, a trilogy of short fables intended to develop children's moral character. He is also a licensed professional counselor in the Chicago area and has advanced degrees in both theology and mental health counseling. Tillman lives with his wife and writing partner, Cheri.

For additional writings by James C. Tillman go to www.bigyellowdogllc.com

We would love to hear from you please contact us at: info@bigyellowdogllc.com